ANTIHERO

☆☆☆

Imperfect Heroes Series
Book 1

C.J. PINARD

ISBN-13: 978-1523651566
ISBN-10: 1523651563

Acknowledgements:

Cover design by: Kellie Dennis @ Book Cover By Design

Dedication:

This is for Emma, queen of the brainstorm.

PROLOGUE

Eight Years Ago

He looked left, then right, trying to ensure the coast was clear. The spray paint can in his right hand heated as his sweaty palm struggled to keep a grip on it. The muggy Florida night hung heavy all around him. He knew wearing a hoodie and jeans in July wasn't smart, yet, he knew he needed to blend into the shadows as easily as possible. He sucked in a breath of humid air and glanced around one more time for assurance. Not seeing anyone, he looked back at his buddies, giving the nod that all was clear. The four of them stepped out of the alley, staying close to the brick wall at the back of the large sports supply mega-store.

A streetlamp that was supposed to project light and protection to the back of the store had long since burned out, and dumpsters were already overflowing with trash. The stench was overwhelming, but they paid it no mind.

As his buddy, Ripper, went to work on the padlock of the grated door barring entrance into the store, he shook the spray can and began to tag the back of the building.

O A B bitches! he wrote in black paint. He stepped

back and looked at it, just as Ripper spoke, breaking him out of the admiration of his handiwork.

"Fuckin' got it!"

He looked over to see Ripper punch the air with his fist, his gloved hand matching his black hoodie. His jeans were dirty and torn, and his designer tennis shoes had seen better days.

He grinned and chucked the spray paint can into the overflowing dumpster. He followed Ripper and the other two inside the store.

All the lights were off, and the store was eerily quiet. The first thing he saw was rows of kayaks up against the entire back wall, their accompanying paddles set neatly in the row holes on each one.

"Hurry up!" Ripper barked, looking back at him and the other two.

Looking up, he stared at the signs hanging from the ceiling, indicating the different departments. He could easily see that they were heading toward the firearms and weapons department. His stomach summersaulted in excitement and nervousness.

The store was dimly lit, but there were a few low lights on throughout, giving them just enough illumination to see around. He turned toward Ripper's voice and saw they were standing at a glass display case full of every kind of gun and weapon you could want. Handguns, shotguns, rifles, crossbows, buck knives, and bows and arrows were displayed beautifully under the glittering glass.

"LT, it's your turn," Ripper said, piercing him with a challenging brown stare, a crowbar held out in front of him.

He looked down at the proffered weapon and then back into Ripper's commanding eyes. Nodding, he took the crowbar and licked his lips before taking a step back, winding the crowbar around like a bat he was ready to hit a homerun with.

"Stand back," he said over his shoulder to the other three.

They took a step back as he swung the crowbar with all his might. An ear-splitting crash filled the quiet store. His elation at breaking the glass on the first try was quickly drowned out by the wailing alarm that followed. A blaring red light accompanied the alarm from out of the gun case, flashing on and off like a police siren.

The store's floodlights soon popped on, and another siren began to screech.

"Oh shit!" Ripper said. "Grab as many as you can and let's get the fuck outta here!"

He didn't need to be told twice. He picked up a smooth black Beretta 9mm and three boxes of bullets. He then shoved the gun into the waistband of his pants and the bullets into the pockets of his hoodie.

Running with all they had toward the back door, the four of them made it into the alley, the warm humid night hitting them in the face as they ran.

Police sirens screamed in the distance, causing their adrenaline to pump even harder until they reached the end of the alley.

"Call you assholes later!" Ripper hollered as the four of them went their separate ways, heading home or wherever they spent their nights.

He yawned and opened his eyes, blinking against the piercing light of the morning sun streaming in through his partially open curtains. Remembering the night before, his eyes flew open and he immediately reached under his pillow to see if his new Beretta was still there. He sighed in relief when his hand wrapped around the warm metal.

Pulling it out, he examined the gun more closely than he had last night. Its black body gleamed in the morning sun. He locked the slide to the rear and looked inside. He fiddled with the magazine release until it fell out into his hand and saw it was empty. He glanced over at his chest of drawers, as he remembered putting the boxes of bullets in his

underwear drawer.

Glancing at his bedroom door, he flipped the thin blanket aside and went over to the chest and slowly opened the top drawer. Moving his underwear aside, he saw the three boxes of 9mm bullets. He breathed a sigh of relief and smiled. He and Ripper and the other two from the OAB had gotten away with it. He was thrilled to have his very own piece to carry around for protection - and when the need arose, intimidation.

"Ellis! Get down here!" he heard his mother call.

He sighed, setting the gun and bullets back into his drawer, covering them up with the undergarments. Pulling on the jeans that were lying in a heap on the floor, he fastened the button and slogged down the stairs.

His mother was in her waitress uniform, spooning hash browns and eggs onto a plate. A cigarette dangled from the corner of her mouth.

"You're going to be late for school," she murmured through a hazy blue cloud of smoke.

He coughed and resisted the urge to wave the smoke away. He loathed the smell and looked forward to the day he could move out of his mother's house.

"I don't give a shit about school," he murmured, squeezing ketchup onto his eggs and hash browns.

He flinched when his mother's palm made

contact with the back of his head. "Boy, you go to school, you graduate, then you can do whatever the hell you want. Until that happens, these are my damn rules. And watch your mouth in my house."

She glared at him before crushing the cigarette out into a nearby ashtray.

He said nothing, just shoveled more food into his mouth, hoping she'd just leave. She headed for the door and opened it. She stepped out into the morning sun, but before closing the door, she pointed a blood-red fingernail at him, her eyes narrowed. "If I get another frickin' call from the school that you've ditched, I'm gonna beat your ass when I get home. You hear me, boy?"

He sucked in a deep breath and nodded. "Yeah, Ma."

"Good."

She slammed the door and Ellis flipped her off after it was closed.

He went to school… barely. He was still hungover from the cheap beer Ripper had manipulated a pretty girl at the corner store to buy for them before they had hit the sports supply store last night.

As he sat at the dining room table staring at his backpack, which was full of homework he most likely wouldn't be doing, he grinned in triumph at his conquest from the night before.

He was in his senior year and wasn't even sure how he'd made it this far. He had continually given each teacher hell every year, learning at an early age that if he was a holy terror in each classroom, the teacher would pass him onto the next grade just to get rid of him.

He startled when the door opened and his mother came walking through, dressed in her uniform, just like she had been that morning.

"Son, how was your day?" she asked.

He looked at her weary blue eyes and wrinkling tanned skin, almost feeling sorry for her. She'd lived a hard life and he knew that he was all she had. Still, he couldn't wait to move away from home and be on his own. She pulled her bleached blonde hair out of its ponytail, set her purse down on a worn kitchen chair, and lit a cigarette.

Sitting at the table with him, she pulled off her rubber shoes and began massaging her feet over the nude-colored pantyhose.

"It was fine, Ma. I got homework, though." He pointed to his backpack.

As she was about to reply, there was a knock on the door to their townhouse.

"You expectin' someone?" she asked through the cigarette at the corner of her mouth.

He shook his head and swallowed hard, trying to think. Ripper hadn't said he was coming by when they'd parted ways at school, and he wasn't expecting anyone else. "No."

She cautiously went to the door, looking through the peephole. She saw two men in suits and ties. Opening the door a crack but leaving the chain bolted, she glared at the two men. "What the hell you want?"

The taller of the two, a clean-cut white guy in a tie, produced a police badge. "Are you Mrs. Anderson?"

She nodded. "Yeah, why?"

"Is there an Ellis Anderson living at this residence? Your son?"

"Yeah."

"We need to speak to him. Now."

Oh, shit, Ellis thought at hearing who was at the door. He thought about running up to his room, throwing the gun and bullets out the window, but what good would that do? They'd find them, and they were covered with his prints. Maybe he could rub the prints off? Maybe he could shimmy up a loose board in his room and hide the contraband under a floorboard. Maybe he could hide them in his laundry basket or the trash can in his bathroom.

Who wants to search through that stuff?

Maybe it was too late and I was completely screwed, he panicked.

His mother briefly closed the door and slid the chain off, opening the door wider and reluctantly inviting the two cops inside. She looked past her decaying porch and down both ways of the street before closing the door, a common habit of most inhabitants of the roughest neighborhood in Orlando.

"Y'all want something to drink?" his mother asked as she awkwardly indicated for them to sit on one of the two sofas, a couple of pink and blue flowered pieces that looked like the 90s might want them back someday.

"No, thank you, Mrs. Anderson," one cop said.

The taller of the two shook his head and looked at Ellis. "You. Come sit over here."

Ellis complied, sitting on the other sofa.

His mother sat on the sofa next to her son and stared at the men.

The one who'd spoken first started. "I'm Detective Atcheson, and this is Detective Johnson." He pointed to his partner, a light-skinned black guy who looked too young to be a cop.

"What's this about?" Mrs. Anderson asked.

Detective Atcheson produced an envelope from

the inside of his suit pocket and set it on his lap. He fixed his stare on Ellis. "Where were you last night, son?"

Ellis swallowed hard, but tried to keep a cool mask over his face. "Out with friends, why?"

"Are you a member of the Orlando Aryan Boys gang?"

He feigned innocence and gasped for effect. "No. No way."

Without warning, the detective reached over and grabbed his arm, yanking his T-shirt sleeve up to expose Ellis's shoulder where a tattoo with the letters "OAB" decorated his shoulder.

His mother gasped. "Ellis John Anderson! How the hell long have you had that?"

Starting to get angry, he yanked his arm away from the detective and pulled his shirt sleeve down. "I got it on my 17th birthday, Ma. Calm down."

"Calm down?" she screeched. "Why are you involved in some gang? I raised you better…"

"With all due respect, Mrs. Anderson, we're here about something more serious than his affiliation with the OAB. The Jensen Sportsman's Warehouse was robbed and vandalized last night, and we know the OAB was responsible."

Ellis and his mother said nothing, just continued to glare at the detectives.

When they didn't respond, the cop cleared his throat and pulled a series of black and white 8 by 10 sized photographs from the envelope he had set on his lap earlier. Spreading them on the wooden coffee table, he pointed at the surveillance video photos and said, "This is you."

It wasn't a question. The detective's hard stare demanded an explanation.

Ellis didn't say anything, he just stared at the photos, wondering how the hell he was gonna get out of this. He absentmindedly wiped his sweaty hands on his jeans. He was brought out of his thoughts when a smack to the back of his head made his vision go fuzzy.

"Answer him now, boy!" his mother ground out, her piercing blue stare shooting daggers at him.

He glanced at her, then back at the detective. "No, that ain't me." He gazed at the photo again, the dark hoodie covering most of his face, only a small part of it was showing. "That could be anyone," he continued, his confidence growing.

The detective nodded, thrusting another photo of him with his arm raised, crowbar in hand, winding up to smash the glass. "This isn't you, either?" The detective was almost mocking him now.

The hoodie had come back a little in the excitement of swinging the crowbar. Ellis sat back and folded his arms. "Nah, not me."

"I see," the detective said, not bothering to show them the rest of the photos, but instead, putting them back into the envelope. He then pulled a piece of paper out of the breast pocket of his suit jacket. He handed it to Ellis's mother. "I have a warrant to search the premises."

Detective Johnson fixed Ellis with a glare. "Unless you'd like to save us the trouble and just tell us where the weapons and ammo are?"

Ellis narrowed his eyes at the detectives. "Fuck you."

"Ellis!" his mother screeched, standing up and yanking him by the arm. "What the hell is going on here?" She was trembling, her eyes a mixture of fear and desperation.

The detectives stood up and tossed the search warrant on the coffee table.

Lifting a shoulder and letting it fall, Detective Atcheson glared at Ellis for his disrespect and then said to his partner while staring at Ellis, "Johnson, you take the kid's room. I'll start in the kitchen."

Just then, two uniformed police officers walked calmly through the front door. "These two will make sure you stay either outside or in this room while we search," Detective Johnson said, heading upstairs.

Not five minutes later, Johnson came down the stairs carrying the gun by its handle in his gloved hand, the boxes of bullets wrapped in a plastic bag. He glared at Ellis, then poked his head into the kitchen, looking at Atcheson, who was pulling drawers and cabinets open. "Found it. Let's roll."

Atcheson spied the gun and then cut his gaze to Ellis, who was on the sofa with his head in his hands. Briskly walking to him, he grabbed his bicep and yanked him up. "Ellis Anderson, you're under arrest for robbery and forced entry."

Ellis pulled out of his grip and began to struggle. He was going to try to flee out of the back door and run - somewhere - *anywhere!* He just had to get out of there.

"Get your fucking hands off me!"

The two armed police officers ran to the aid of the detective and pinned the boy to the floor, putting handcuffs on behind his back.

"Get off me!" Ellis screamed again. "Let me go!"

They stood him up as he continued to struggle futilely.

"Don't make me taze you, boy," said one of the officers, a large guy who looked like he'd been a professional linebacker before he became a cop. His hand was twitching to pull out his Taser and his face was stern and serious.

They escorted Ellis to the front door, Detective Johnson opening it for them.

"No, please don't take my boy, please!" his mother pled, falling to her knees, sobbing.

"Sorry, ma'am," Atcheson said, cutting her a sympathetic glance. He walked over and pulled a card from his breast pocket, offering it to her. "Here's my contact info. Call me tomorrow and I'll tell you if he's made bail."

She continued to cry, tears streaming down her cheeks, ignoring the detective. He placed the card on the coffee table and the detectives and officers left with Ellis in custody, placing him in the back of a police cruiser.

"This is your third strike, Mr. Anderson," the judge said, his wise hazel eyes narrowing on the defendant as he sat in the Orange County, Florida courtroom.

Ellis simply nodded as his court-appointed attorney leaned over and whispered something in his ear.

His mother was seated behind them in the galley, clutching her purse and watching in horror as the judge handed down a sentence to her only child.

The judge cleared his throat and looked at the paper in front of him, his glasses perched on his nose as the arms of his black robe swept across the desk as he read. He lifted his eyes up to Ellis. Removing his glasses, he set the paper down and folded his hands over it. "You know, when you first appeared in front of me last year, I gave you a chance, like I do to all teens. I thought maybe you were on the wrong path and that some community service helping the homeless would open your eyes. But no. Six months later you appeared again in front of me, on yet another robbery charge. Boy, the worst thing you could have ever done is get involved with the Orlando Aryan Boys. The other three are already behind bars, and your leader," he looked down at his paper, "Justin Silver - or 'Ripper', is going to have a hell of a time in prison with the other gang bangers. But you," he sighed, "I still don't think you are beyond repair, even though you seem to be on the same path as your father." He shook his head. "Despite that, your mother has tried her hardest to raise you, but you've continued to disappoint her, time after time, haven't you?"

Ellis cut his eyes down to the desk, unable to look at the judge. As much of a hard-ass as he'd become, he still hated that he'd hurt his mother. "Answer me, boy!" the judge roared, pounding his fist on the large oak desk in front of him.

His eyes darted to the judge and nodded. "Yes, sir."

"Well, I'm going to do you a huge favor today."

Ellis, his mother, his attorney, and the entire courtroom were silent, hanging on every word coming from the judge's mouth.

"Instead of prison, you are to enlist in the United States Marine Corps, effective immediately. You want to play with guns and pretend to be a tough guy? Let's see how you handle the toughest boot camp in the world, and maybe a deployment or two."

Ellis's eyes got big, and he bit back a curse. "But–"

The judge cut him off. "Shut up, boy, I'm not done."

Ellis's jaw ticked with defiance, but he just simply nodded.

"If you do not complete four full years of active enlistment, you will be brought back here to Orange County, where you will serve a term of no less than seven years in a state penitentiary of my choosing."

Ellis's attorney raised a hand. "Your honor, the boy is only 17, and has not finished high school. I don't believe the military will accept him without a high school diploma."

The judge nodded. "Right. He will take a G.E.D. test, which he *will* pass, and that will satisfy their enlistment qualifications. If he doesn't pass it, this one-time get-out-of-jail-free-card is null and void, and he will be off to prison - where, by the way," he looked at Ellis, "they make you get your G.E.D. anyway, so keep that mind, boy. You hear me?" The judge narrowed his eyes at the defendant.

"I do, sir," Ellis eked out, swallowing hard.

The judge pounded his gavel and shook his graying head. "Court adjourned."

Chapter 1

Ellis

Present Day

If pain is weakness leaving the body, then what is it called when pain leaves the heart?

The fact that the gang I'd joined when I was 17 had called me "LT" turned out to be a sort of twisted poetic justice. The "leader" - if you could call him that, Ripper, had said Ellis was a stupid name and said LT sounded close enough. Then he made me "First Lieutenant" of the OAB. A title, at the time, I was proud to have.

Now, it just confused people - or it did during my eight years in the Marines. LT is the nickname for 'lieutenant' there too, but I hadn't been a lieutenant in the Corps. No, those were the college-educated types. I'd started out as a grunt and made my way to First Sergeant by the time my tenure was up. Yes, the judge had sentenced me to four years, but by the grace of God, that judge, to whom I owed my life, had known what he was doing. He had seen something in me that not I, or even my mother, had seen in me: Potential. Instead of being the bad kid with the pretty face I'd appeared to be on the outside, I was actually a good kid just in with an ugly crowd. A sadly typical story, one that, fortunately, did not have a tragic ending. So I ended up serving another 4 years because I wanted to, not because I had to this time.

Well, some might say it could still end that way, but not me.

My past sins have definitely come back to haunt me. Not the sins of my teenaged youth; no, not those. Petty theft and robbery is nothing compared to what I've done and seen during my awesome, wonderful, sad, horrible, and terrific time in the United States Marine Corps.

The horrors, the triumphs, the defeats, the victories, they're all wrapped up in one big confusing ball of memories and nightmares. The places I've seen, the people I've met, the women I've loved and let go, the brothers and friends I've loved and lost... all worth every moment. Even if I did come out of that part of my life scathed, scarred, broken, put back together, and then broken again.

There are times, when I'm alone, that I fight against the memories, battle against a breakdown at what I've been through, and then five or ten minutes later, I'm laughing like an idiot at a memory. Something that really isn't funny, it's just amusing to me, forever burned in my brain.

I have scars on the inside and the outside, and you know what? Thank you, Judge Perkins, because

I wouldn't trade them for an easier life. The mark that digs the deepest, though, isn't one you can see. The one *she* left on my fucking soul.

Out of all the horrible battle scars I've endured… the cuts, bruises, gashes, abrasions, torn muscles, and sprains, the most softest and gentlest of the species has left the harshest mark, the largest ache, the most gaping wound. It was the most comical contradiction on the planet, and if I could take it back, I wouldn't.

Talia

Strength is more than muscles and brawn. It's the resolve to say "no" with your mouth when your heart and the rest of your body want to say, "Yes, yes! God, yes!"

I stared at the customer, a fake smile plastered on my face as she looked down at her smartphone. Growing tired of her ignoring me, I kept the painful smile on and said, "Ma'am, I'm gonna need you to order, or else I can take the person behind you while you decide?"

She looked up from her phone, her perfectly

manicured finger paused over the screen. "Oh, sorry," she bit out with her annoyingly beautiful red lips. I watched as she pursed them together, and I rubbed my palm against my green apron to keep from balling up my fist. She looked up at the menu board behind me, then back down at her phone. "I'll take a chai latte, no foam, no sugar," she finally said, not even bothering to make eye contact.

I punched her order into the register computer with more annoyance than I meant to and said, "That's three-fifty-two."

Not sure she heard me, and while smiling in apology to the customers waiting behind her, I looked back at the stupid blondie in front me and repeated, "Ma'am, that's three-fifty-two."

She looked up, bright blue eyes piercing me with annoyance as if I'd interrupted her text. "Oh, sorry." She looked back down at her phone and punched a few buttons, then slid the phone under the scanner to pay for the drink with her app.

Damn yuppies. I hate them all.

"Do you need a receipt?" I asked, biting the inside of my cheek 'til I could swear I tasted blood.

She dismissed me with a wave, her eyes still on her phone, and walked to the other side of the counter. I looked at the screen to find her name from her payment information and wrote it on the cup. I set it on the counter with her order written on it. I purposely misspelled "Jennifer" just to piss her off.

I took some calming breaths in order to be nice to the poor customers who had been just as much a victim to Jennifer's rudeness as I had.

Thankfully, the shift passed quickly and without any more asshole customers. When 9 p.m. finally rolled around, I yanked off my apron and hung it up in the back room. I couldn't grab my purse and call out a goodbye to my coworkers fast enough. I got into my little car and drove toward home.

As I reached my apartment complex, my phone chirped with a text. I killed the engine and looked around the parking lot before checking my phone.

Ellis: *You home?*

I sighed. I knew what Ellis wanted. He wanted to come over and bring some wine and beer and maybe a pizza and pretend to want to watch movies all under the pretense of a casual night inside. But I knew what would happen, we'd barely touch the pizza, have too much to drink, and he'd pierce me with his sky blue eyes and then run his fingers through his short black hair and then kiss me. Then he'd tell me he how hot I was, and I'd giggle. Then he'd do it again, and soon his talented and wandering hands would find their way under my shirt. This was all a prelude to a long night of sweaty, mind-blowing sex, which ended in the morning with him gone before sunrise and me wondering what I had done wrong, questioning everything about myself. Then I wouldn't hear from him for another week or so.

That was a vicious cycle I'd lived for over six months, and I most certainly wasn't going to repeat it, no matter how damn hot Ellis Anderson was.

I gazed down at his text, contemplating not replying, but that never worked either. If I didn't respond, he'd just show up.

If I replied and told him to come over, he would be here in ten minutes.

If I told him I was busy, or tired, or had to be at class early tomorrow, he'd show up anyway.

So I tried a tactic I hadn't tried before. I didn't want to resort to this, but the guy was relentless – and aggressive.

Me: *I'm not alone. Sorry, guy. Maybe some other time.*

I gazed at my reply, mustering up the courage to hit 'send.'

"Ah, screw it," I said, pressing the green icon to send the text. I shoved the phone in my purse, hoping its battery would die before I'd have to suffer the repercussions of his reply. A small grin bent my lips as I imagined his ridiculously handsome face twisting into surprise when he read my reply.

Screw him. He's a user. My heart can't handle his games.

I put my key into the lock of my meager apartment and sighed in relief. My cat, Misty, was immediately winding herself around my legs, meowing for food. I bent down and picked her up.

I threw my purse on the coffee table and scratched behind her black pointed ears and popped her on her white nose with my finger. "You miss me today, girl? Huh?"

I carried her over to the kitchen where I pulled out a can of cat food and pried the top off, dumping it into her food bowl. I then filled her water dish to the brim from the tap and set it back down. Misty went to town gobbling down her food while I went into my room to change.

Smiling as I heard my phone chiming with texts, I changed into some loose white shorts and an oversized orange and white T-shirt which read NOT A MORNING PERSON and went back out to the kitchen.

Opening the fridge, I spied some leftover Italian food. I quickly dumped it onto a plate and shoved it into the microwave, starting the thing up and waiting for it to do its job.

I sighed at how tired I was. Why the hell was that stupid coffee shop open 'til 9 p.m. anyway? I had to be at my morning class by 8 a.m. and that sucked, since I had a test in the morning and hadn't studied yet.

When the microwave beeped, I pulled the plate from it and plucked a water bottle from the fridge, setting both down at my dining room table. My backpack was on the floor and I pulled out the big History book. Thumbing to the appropriate page, I began reading, trying my hardest to absorb the information for the Civil War test I had tomorrow.

My phone chirping again broke my concentration. With my noodles paused at my lips, I sighed in annoyance and set my fork down. I got up and yanked my phone from my purse, not wanting to read the texts but doing it anyway.

Ellis: *I know you're lying. U don't have some guy over there.*

I laughed at that one. Of course I hadn't responded in 2.2 seconds so he sent another: *You're just trying to make me jealous.*

I laughed again.

The next one read: *I'm coming over, and if there is some guy there, I'm gonna throat punch him, so he better be gone by the time I get there.*

Geez! What is his problem?

Ellis and I had met at my coffee shop. It's set right outside the largest military base in Tampa, and we get all kinds of servicemen and women in there. The day Ellis walked in, my breath had caught in my throat, and I'd found it hard to concentrate on the other customers and their orders.

There were three people in front of him in line. He was wearing jeans and a fitted red USMC T-shirt that hugged his every ridge and muscle. His crystal blue eyes were studying the menu board with his arms folded over his hard chest, his black hair was cut into that short military style. He stood perfectly still and I was having a hard time giving the other customers my full attention like they deserved. My palms were sweating by the time he reached the front of the line.

"Hi," I said. "What can I get you?"

His eyes drilled into mine. "Just a black coffee, sweetheart."

My heart dropped into my stomach. I swallowed hard at the sound of his deep, sexy voice. "Do you need room for cream?"

His lips twitched in amusement. "No. No cream in my coffee."

My pale cheeks burned red at the innuendo and I tried my hardest to plaster on my professional smile. "You got it." I remember winking at him, and at the time, thinking about how uncharacteristic it was of me to flirt like that.

"That's a dollar-eight-five," I had told him.

He handed me two one-dollar bills and when I handed him his fifteen cents in change, our hands briefly touched and I suddenly got tingly at the connection. He tossed the coins into the tip jar and shoved an additional dollar in while not breaking eye contact with me.

So flustered, I had forgotten to ask him something important as he went to walk away. "Uh, what name?"

"LT," he'd answered.

I nodded and wrote L.T. on the cup. I also put my name and cell phone number underneath it in yet another uncharacteristically bold move on my part.

LT was the name the barista had called out when his order was ready, and it didn't go unnoticed by me that a lot of the patrons of the store looked up when they'd called out his name. They had all stared at him in curiosity when he'd picked up his coffee.

Before leaving the store, I watched as he squinted at what was printed on the cup. He grinned in amusement and lifted it in greeting to me before exiting the store, rumbling out of the parking lot on some loud motorcycle.

So hot.

Chapter 2

Ellis

Rage was burning a hole in my stomach. She better not have anyone over at her place. I'll kill him. I swear to God, I'll fucking kill him. Nobody touches Talia. Nobody but me.

My car came to a screeching halt in the parking lot of her apartment complex. I got out, arming the alarm and charging up to her door, knocking with more force than necessary.

It felt like an eternity until she opened the door. In the meantime, I was ready to break it down. My teeth ground together as I waited for the door to open. As soon as I saw her, all my rage melted into a warm puddle in my chest. Her long, red curls were sitting to one side over her delicate shoulder and she was wearing a thin orange T-shirt with an obnoxious saying on it. The short-shorts she wore showed off her creamy, long-stem legs.

"Don't you take a hint?" she said, her lips in a firm, grim line, but her light brown eyes glittering with excitement and amusement.

I pushed the white door open and heard its smack against the plaster of the wall.

"Well, why don't you come in?" she murmured

dryly.

My eyes darted around the apartment, coming to land on the empty plate and fork set next to the large textbook perched on her small dining room table. Her cat, Misty, meowed at me before curling herself around my legs.

I looked down at the cat, knowing that if anyone else was in the apartment, she'd be coiled up in his or her lap, as she was the most emotional, needy cat *ever*.

"Why you wind me up like that, T?" I asked, my arms folded over my chest as she rested her luscious ass on the edge of the dining room table, her arms matching my posture across her chest.

I used all my willpower to keep my eyes on hers. "Answer me."

She snorted and waved her hand, pushing off the table and making her way around it to go sit down in front of the textbook.

Annoyed, I crossed the distance between us and grabbed her hand before she could sit, pulling her to me and pressing her soft body against mine. "Not so fast. You haven't answered my question."

She scoffed and pushed away, although I noticed a hesitation for a split second. "I don't owe you shit."

"Dammit," I said, raking my fingers through my hair. "You can't do that to me. Just tell me you want to be alone or something."

She threw her head back and laughed, sitting down at the table. "Yeah, right. I've tried it all, Ellis. You don't listen and won't listen. You're a stubborn-ass mule." She shook her head.

I shoved my keys into my jeans pocket, the red and gold USMC lanyard dangling out. "The fuck that's supposed to mean?"

She sighed and shoved the pencil behind her ear. It was a sexy-as-hell move and I tried to ignore it as I stared into her defiant eyes. "You know what it means. You want me when you want me, but when you don't, nobody else can have me."

I cocked my head to the side, confused at her words, because I wanted her *all* of the time. "What are you talking about?"

She narrowed her eyes and bit her cherry red lip. "Just go, Ellis." She gestured around her small apartment. "As you can see, there's nobody else here. I've got a big test tomorrow, and I don't need you keeping me up all hours."

I stared at her incredulously. "You're not serious."

Her teeth still had her bottom lip hostage and it made my cock twitch in my pants when she did that. "I'm very serious."

"Can't I just stay for a little while?" I threw her my sexy smirk and pleading eyes.

A look I couldn't quite decipher passed over her features. It bordered between annoyed and turned on. She must have seen my expression and looked down at her book again. She pulled the pencil from behind her ear and put it to her mouth. "Just go, please."

I stood there for a few long seconds, staring at her, but she wouldn't look up. Giving up, I left her place, quietly closing her door behind me and getting into my car.

As I drove home, I couldn't understand what had happened. I wanted her - and I could tell she wanted me, too. This was our way. Whenever I'd call, she would be there. So why hadn't she been there when I'd needed her? What was her problem tonight?

For the first few months after we'd met, we were inseparable. She'd come to my place or I'd be at her little apartment with her and her needy black cat. But in the past few weeks, she'd sort of grown distant. I didn't understand it at all. All I'd asked is that she not fuck anyone else. That she was mine and mine alone. I didn't understand what was so hard about that.

Admittedly – releasing from the service had been hard on me. I never liked to admit weakness but having to go back to being a civilian after being owned by the government for so long took some adjustment. I was actively looking for a job in the "real world" while collecting some government money after being in for so long, but I was mostly going out on the weekends and having fun.

I was 25 now, probably time for me to calm the hell down and get some sort of career going for myself, but I was tired. One on hand, I wanted to rest and try to take my time in finding a job, but the other half me, the one who was used to being busy and following orders, was becoming restless.

At the stoplight, I rolled the window down and let the warm night air wash into the car. With my head tilted back against the headrest, I scrubbed a hand over the scruff on my chin and cheeks. Admittedly, it was nice to grow it out a little instead of having to have it baby-ass smooth every day for inspection. I planned on growing my hair out a little bit, too.

I spied the pack of cigarettes lying on the floorboard of the passenger side and contemplated leaning over and picking them up and having one. I'd vowed to quit when I got out of the service, and I pretty much had, but I still wanted one occasionally.

A loud honk blaring from behind me blew that

idea.

Looking in my rearview mirror, the angry driver behind me had his hands flailing around and honked again. I could hear him cussing me out through my open window and looked at the light. It was green, but we were also the only two people on the street.

What the fuck?

This guy was pissing me off.

I should have just hit the gas, but instead, I shoved the car into park. I flung open my door and got out, storming toward him. His eyes got big seeing me come at him, and miraculously, he'd stopped yelling and making hand gestures at me.

I watched as his window zipped up and he yanked the steering wheel to the right and pealed out and around my car to zoom through the light.

"That's what I thought, asshole! Could have just gone around me earlier, you dick!" I put up both middle fingers toward his retreating piece of shit Honda.

I shook my head and got back into my car. Damn, it would have been nice to have cracked his skull. Or at least have roughed him up a little.

Reaching down to the passenger floorboard, I grabbed the cigarettes and pulled one from the pack and pushed the car's lighter in to heat it up. Shoving the unlit cigarette behind my ear, I put the car in gear and proceeded to go, even though the light had turned red again.

Good thing the streets were empty. The lighter popped and I lit my addiction stick with it and took a drag. Thinking of the asshole who'd sped away earlier, I smiled, cigarette dangling from the corner of my mouth. Just like my mother used to - and I'd hated it when she did that. Now look at me.

Chapter 3
Talia

"I aced my History final!" I squealed to my friend and boss, Bo.

She hugged me. "That's so great! I'm so proud of you, sweetie!"

Bo - or Bonita, the full, formal name she never used - had been a good friend and huge cheerleader of mine since my darker days. She had gotten me the job at the coffee shop and encouraged me to go back to school. She was currently managing the shop while trying to raise two daughters alone, and I admired her strength.

When her (now ex) husband had put her in the ICU with a few broken bones and facial swelling that made her almost unrecognizable, I had crumpled in grief when I'd visited her at the hospital. I couldn't believe a human being could do that to another. I'd held her hand while she cried, and had driven her home from the hospital when she'd been strong enough to leave.

Watching her struggle to pay for a divorce attorney and restraining order and remain strong for her daughters gave me the strength I needed to break the addiction I was currently living with. An addiction that had been the demise of my mother, one that had made me so angry at her. And there I was, following in her footsteps, a path I most certainly didn't need to be taking.

After getting her life together, Bo had told me sternly it was time for me to get clean. I had only been 21 at the time, and she saw some potential in me that I hadn't seen in myself. She showed me that strength came in all forms, and when she helped me get clean, I felt like I finally had family again, even if she wasn't blood. And in my case, blood most certainly wasn't thicker than water.

Breaking my addiction to cocaine was the single hardest thing I'd ever done. Not even burying my mother or watching my father leave out the front door with a suitcase in his hand when I was 10 years old was harder. No. Breaking a drug addiction was the worst pain of my life.

The day before I'd entered rehab, I made sure to go out with a bang. I'd snorted all the coke I could get my hands on, then I drank a shitload of whiskey and whatever else they had at the party I'd gone to. I woke a couple days later lying next to some dude on the floor of the house I'd been partying at. He looked in as bad of shape as me.

I don't even remember how I got home early that morning. I really don't. The suitcase lying open and empty on my bed sobered me up pretty fast, though. With a banging headache, a few trips to the porcelain god to throw up, and cottonmouth from hell, I had packed that suitcase and called Bo to tell her I was ready to go. Even though my hands were shaking something fierce and tears were beginning to form in my eyes.

She'd dropped me off at the New Beginnings Treatment Center here in Tampa and I had been terrified the first day - which didn't turn out to be so bad. I was shown to a room, and then to where the dining hall was. By the end of that first night, I was sad and down, but okay, my resolve strong.

I woke the next morning in pain. I was shaking even worse and it felt like all my nerve endings were on fire. They were crying out for the drug they were so used to getting, but I was depriving them of it.

"It hurts," I'd sobbed to the counselor. "It hurts bad. Can't you give me something?" I'd asked, begging her for mercy.

She'd looked at me with kind, mocha colored eyes and skin the color of chocolate and had shook her head. "I'm sorry, sweetie, no."

Then came the profuse vomiting and the sweating as the drug worked itself out of my system. It had been so bad, I'd almost passed out from the pain. I had cried and pulled my hair out until it lay in pieces on the bathroom floor. I had tried to be strong but eventually succumbed to sleep, and I think I slept for two days straight after that.

When I woke, I felt better. I attempted to eat a little and tried to distract myself with TV, reading, and talking to the other residents. I had been proud I'd gone through the worst, but little did I know, the worst was yet to come. I had another 27 days to get through without anything stronger than aspirin.

I shook my head at the memory. It plagued me night and day. I had never told another living soul except Bo.

"You're almost there, baby girl," Bo said, shoving a cupful of ground espresso into the machine and pushing the start button.

I wiped my hands on my apron and filled a paper cup with steaming hot, dark coffee from the tall, stainless-steel container, then I secured a plastic lid on top.

"I know. I'm so close. I just wish I knew what kind of job I wanted after I got my degree."

She smirked at me while dumping a shot glass of espresso into a larger plastic cup filled with something white and foamy. "You'll figure it out. You're bright and ridiculously smart."

I grinned a little. She was so good at charming people, at making people smile. It was why she made manager of this store so quickly. She had the ability to smile through her pain and put on a pretty, happy face, even when she wanted to die.

Those were her words, not mine, but I could relate.

My phone vibrated in my apron pocket and I waited until there were no more customers in my line before walking into the back room to check it. It was a text from Ellis.

U busy tonight? I need to see your beautiful red-headed self.

I sighed. My night was wide open and the thought of seeing him exhilarated me a little, but also scared me. I was supposed to be distancing myself from him, because he just wasn't good for me. So if I let him in and he hurt me, I had nobody to blame but myself.

Still, my heart ached at the thought of seeing him. I'd told him to leave a few nights ago. But he obviously knew this dysfunctional connection between us was still very, very strong. I bit my lip in contemplation. Do I want to have him just for a night, his body next to mine, his breath in my ear, his sexy, deep voice dripping words from a talented tongue that I knew was mere lip service by a set of beautiful, perfect lips, just to have the pain of my bed being empty come morning?

Yes, yes I did.

So I responded to him: Sorry, baby. Maybe some other night.

The fact that I wanted him made me turn him down to spare me the heartache. The fact that I called him baby just to keep him hanging on was my insecurity showing. Maybe I was just as much of an asshole as he was. Oh, the games we play.

The next night was nothing different. He'd actually not texted back last night, but today, he was back at it. I was on the closing shift again today, and the texts from him started late afternoon:

I can't stay away from you much longer, beautiful.

I'm coming over tonight, and you're going to be happy when I arrive. Trust me.

I rolled my eyes at his attempt at charm. I had just taken my last final today and had a glorious two weeks off until next semester. I wouldn't get home 'til late, but that never stopped him before. I wanted to see him – I always wanted to see him – but I knew I shouldn't.

However, that didn't stop me from texting him back and telling him I was free.

Why did I do that?

Ellis: *What time you get off?*

Me: *9*

Ellis: *I'll be over at 9:15.*

I bit my lip again. I knew why he was coming over. It was the only reason he ever came over. But I missed him, even if I was stupid and shouldn't be. I needed to find myself another guy. Get into a "real" relationship with someone who wasn't so messed up. Not that I wasn't screwed up myself, but two messy people trying to love each other was not going to work. I needed a normal guy who would worship me and buy me jewelry with his good-paying job. Not this scarred-up dude who didn't know how to express his emotions and said "fuck" too much.

My reply: See you then.

See? I'm no better than he is. We're both a steaming, scorching, hot mess… together.

Ellis

Looking at the computer, I wondered what kind of job I should get. The job I'd had in the Marine Corps was what I'd loved, but I really didn't learn anything much except how to kill people quickly and how to shoot a bunch of different types of weapons. That, and how to disassemble and reassemble a rifle in less than a minute. Something told me this wasn't a skill that would get me a very high paying job. After all, who uses weapons? Military and law enforcement. I'd already done the military, and after my stint as a teen in the OAB and my arrests, there was no way I was getting a job in law enforcement. Not that I really wanted one. I'd always had some sort of aversion to cops. Probably my rebellious nature. They made me nervous.

I smirked a little at that, knowing in the back of my mind that it was wrong and stupid, but I couldn't help it. My mom knew it, too, which is why I rarely heard from her anymore. She'd gotten remarried about two years after I joined, and I was glad she had someone to take care of her. Even as a teen I had always felt like I should be looking out for her, even though back then I mostly just looked out for myself and my homies, because I was a stupid, selfish, misguided kid. Trying to fit in where I could get in, and not caring about the repercussions or how it would impact my mom, my family, or anyone else around me.

I slammed the laptop lid closed with a sigh and scrubbed a hand over my face. Gazing around my small little mobile home, I looked at my keys lying on my kitchen counter. A smile lit up my face.

Maybe a bike ride would help my mood?

Getting up from the chair, I plucked up my keys and headed out to the parking lot. The Florida sun was blazing overhead, and the wind was warm and muggy.

Slinging my leg over my beautiful black and blue Ducati Diavel, I pushed the engine to start and rumbled out of the parking lot of my apartment complex.

I should technically be wearing a helmet, but, well, fuck that. My sunglasses helped to keep the wind out of my eyes so I could see and I felt freer weaving in and out of the downtown traffic as I made my way toward the beach highway. I heard a few honks as I wound my way through the cars, and I responded with my customary one-finger greeting, along with my accompanying cocky-ass grin.

I seemed to be able to breathe again as my bike and I reached the 275 freeway so I could ride across the bridge and clear my head as the crystal blue waters glistened under the sun. Testing the throttle, I pushed it harder than it should be pushed and my bike made a beautiful sound as it ate pavement across the bridge.

I wasn't much to admire beauty of any kind, but the gulf coast waters made anyone who crossed their paths appreciate them. Only two other beautiful things ever made me pause. One was the smell of gunpowder after obliterating a target on shooting day, and the pearly white smile of a redhead who had flipped my life upside down.

I couldn't explain why Talia did the things she did to me, but all I knew was that I had tried to look for another girl, I had tried sleeping with randoms I'd meet here and there, but none of them were *her*. Not even motherfucking close.

The sky and sea passed me in a blur as I continued to ride, hoping to find some sea-lined highway I could just fly down without a care in the world. But even I knew that wasn't entirely true. I would always have cares in the world, but sometimes I wanted to forget them.

Forget that I needed to probably find a job, and soon.

Forget that I, most likely, would never sleep a full 7 or 8 hours a night uninterrupted by nightmares again for the rest of my days.

Forget that the missing finger on my left hand would never be coming back.

Forget that, despite all of the above, I would never care for anyone other than Talia ever again. I'd tried and I'd failed and now I had to figure out a way to tell her. She played games with me, and I didn't know if it was because she was just a player herself, or because she was scared of me - of us - on some level.

I wanted to "wine and dine" her. I wanted to show her off to the world and let her meet my mom and new stepdad. But I didn't know how to broach that conversation. I didn't know how to do anything but strip her bare and love her with my body and feel her body loving mine back. I always wished that would be enough, but with what little I knew about women, I just knew it wouldn't and couldn't be.

There were friends of mine in the service who were married. Their beautiful wives seemed to be perfect for them. I should have asked them back then how they met and kept their wives. Because as of now, I was failing on a serious level and I didn't know to bring up my score.

I had taken her out several times, but lately it seemed like all she did was work and go to school - and trust me, I was proud of her for going to school. Lord knows I couldn't. It's not that I didn't want to better myself; it was just that I didn't think I could. I was never very book-smart, but working with my hands in figuring out the intricacies on how things worked had always been my specialty. I'd driven my mother crazy as a kid because I would take random things apart - like clocks and phones - to see how they worked.

While I was glad Talia kept busy with her studies, she just didn't seem to have time to go out with me, so I took what I could get from her. A few hours here, a few hours there - but one thing remained the same: Every minute spent with her was passionate and unforgettable. She and I were a blend of the right chemistry that melded together into the perfect mixture. Or perhaps it was just a perfect storm we were brewing.

I soon found myself flying down the coastline, feeling awesome but wanting to see my girl something fierce all of a sudden. I took the next exit to get some gas and an energy drink. I'd text her once I stopped to see what she was doing tonight. I needed her right now for some reason.

Chapter 4
Talia

Once I walked into the house, I fed Misty and set my purse down, just as my phone chirped inside it.

Ellis: *I'm 15 minutes out.*

I smirked and plugged the phone into its charger on the wall in the kitchen.

Did I want Ellis coming over?

Maybe.

No, not maybe. I *so* did, even though I knew he'd just be gone in the morning. A morning where I would really love for him to be here with me, reassuring me that he'd wanted to be here with me, but I knew that most likely wouldn't happen.

I took a quick shower to wash off the coffee smell that seemed to have permeated my every pore, and wondered what I should wear. I rubbed some jasmine-scented lotion on my body and pulled on a fitted hot-pink tank top with some black yoga pants.

Even though he was on his way, I didn't bother to put on any makeup or do anything with my hair. It was currently lying in a mass of damp, unruly waves on my shoulders as I grabbed the remote and popped the TV on.

The reality show I'd been watching had barely just started when my doorbell rang. I stiffened up in nervousness and took a deep breath, turning the TV off and getting up to answer the door.

Oh, God.

My knees went weak and I almost crumpled to the floor at the sight of him. Ellis stood there grinning, his dark hair was a little messy, and he had some stubble on his chin. His black leather jacket was slung over the shoulder of his white T-shirt, and resting against the thigh of his jeans he held his sunglasses.

Placing a cool smile on my face, I opened the door wider and indicated for him to come in.

He immediately dropped the helmet and jacket on my couch and turned around and looked at me. Stalking toward me hungrily, he wrapped his arms around my hips and lifted me up, pressing me flush against his hard body. His lips covered mine and I sighed into his mouth as he began really kissing me. Hungry, desperate, passionate.

I wrapped my legs around his waist as he placed both hands under each of my ass cheeks possessively, walking us joined together into the bedroom, his mouth still devouring mine.

He playfully tossed me on the bed. I landed on my back with a giggle, watching his all-too serious face as he placed one knee on the bed and reached up with both hands, yanking my yoga pants off in one pull.

No I had no panties on. I mean, why bother?

He reached one hand over his shoulder to his back, yanking the plain white tee off over his head and then he tossed it to the floor. With a wicked grin, he climbed all the way onto the bed. When both his hands slid up my bare stomach to push the tank top up and over my head, I giggled like a schoolgirl. The only light on in my bedroom came from the adjoining bathroom light, which was enough to illuminate the room a little. I now lay there bare, raw, exposed, and not giving one single care at my nakedness.

His eyes raked over my body in greedy appreciation. "So damn beautiful."

I was glad he couldn't see the red stain creep up my cheeks as the compliment rushed straight from my ears to my heart. I had never been told I was beautiful or even pretty very much in my life, and every time he said it, it never got old.

His hard body was now pressing against mine. He leaned down and licked my collarbone, switching to kisses until he reached the sensitive spot under my jawline. The sensation was driving me insane with desire.

Ellis kissed me once - hard and desperate - on

the mouth. He pulled off of me, grabbing one ankle and flipping me over on my stomach. Once I felt his weight press the bed down, I knew what was coming next. He'd wedge a knee against one of mine and force my legs open and make love to me deliciously hard. Not that he had to do that much work, I was already open and ready for him.

To my happy surprise, instead of his cock pressing against me, his soft, warm tongue started working at the very top of my sex and then slowly lathed down to the bottom. Except he was on his knees, both hands gripping my ass as his tongue did things that made me whimper with desire. When he had made one full lap up, he worked back down, the rough but soft texture of his mouth causing me to cry out.

Putting a finger into me, he bent it slightly, rubbing perfectly against my G-spot, the pad of his thumb simultaneously pushing erotically at my clit in small circles. I held my breath and tried not to let loose so quickly. I was so turned on, so swollen and ready, but my stubborn side didn't want him to know how badly. I breathed through the sensations of what he was doing, his hard, warm body pressed up against me. I could feel and hear him breathing close behind me, and when he said, "Damn, baby, you're so wet," it only took a few of his well-placed strokes and I was screaming at the top of my lungs. The orgasm ripped through me, my whole body shaking while Ellis's fingers continued to rub every magic spot I had.

My body and mind then began to have a tug-of-war. My body wanted to collapse into a boneless heap onto the bed, but the promise of what his cock could do to me began to overtake my sex-clouded mind. With my whole body still trembling, I began to pull myself up when I felt rough and talented hands grip both my hipbones, pulling my backside up until my ass was in the air. I heard him suck in a breath at the sight. Then I felt his palm smoothly rub over the sensitive skin of my right ass cheek, massaging it gently, moaning in appreciation. He smacked it lightly, and then I heard him stand and remove his jeans, then the distinct sound of a foil wrapper being opened as he put the condom on. Then the sharp sting of another slap on my ass reverberated throughout the room and I gasped at the pleasurable pain it induced. Before I'd had a chance to take another breath and admit to myself that I was nowhere near done, he was suddenly slamming inside of me with a deep, guttural moan synchronized with his forceful thrust.

My eyes rolled back as I cried out at the delicious intrusion. I involuntarily arched my spine so my backside was farther up, allowing him to push in even deeper. One of his hands remained gripped around my hipbone while the other reached around to touch my most sensitive spot gently. His fingertips brushed both himself and me while he continued his forceful, aggressive strokes in and out.

My head was jerked back, face upturned at the ceiling at the feeling of what he was doing with those fingers. Pleasure began to build inside me again like a tidal wave. I felt him move his hand from my hipbone, up the flat of my stomach, and to my bare breast, where his magical fingers began to do things to my hardened, sensitive bud that was driving me insane. I cried out, greedily needing another release.

"Come all over me, baby," Ellis whispered, his words guttural, needy.

I began to pant at his words, feeling like I couldn't breathe, my world going dark as I closed my eyes. A mounting desire began to form too quickly inside me, my stomach sucking in to stave off the desire for just a few seconds longer. My sex clenched, dripping and swollen against his beautiful cock and what it was doing to me. It didn't take me long to shatter under his skilled thrusts, gripping the sheets and screaming out his name and a few shouts to God as I rode out the blinding orgasm. His dick was doing things to my insides that rivaled what his fingers were doing to my outsides - my peaked buds, the swollen need between my legs. As I clenched around him, he too pushed against me hard, stilling as his body pulsed, both hands now clasping my hips almost painfully as he groaned his release into me, laying his hard chest against my back. He collapsed on top of me, breathing hard into my ear. He didn't lie there long, but rolled over, got rid of the condom, then came back to lie down next to me.

I had rolled over onto my back and threw my tank top back over my head, pulling it down to cover half my exposed body. The covers were pulled up to the flat of my stomach. As Ellis climbed in, his warmth radiated onto me, causing me to sigh in happiness.

The sex with him was great, obviously - and his visits here and there were all I had. Was he a commitment-phobe? I didn't know. Would he be here in the morning when I woke? He never had been. Did I care? Of course I did. Was there anything I could do to change the outcome? I was too tired to care. I drifted off into a satisfied, blissful sleep.

Chapter 5

Ellis

God, she looked so beautiful lying there asleep. Her red hair was splayed out over the crisp, white pillow, and the light from the electronics in the room caused the shadow of her eyelashes to illuminate over her cheeks as her eyes were closed and peaceful.

But I had to go. I didn't want her to wake up and find me there. I suppose I should rephrase that. I didn't *think* she wanted me there when her beautiful caramel colored eyes fluttered open in the morning and saw me still lingering. Talia was a strong girl. She didn't seem like the type who would want to find a man in her bed at 8 in the morning as the sun was streaming into her windows. She would probably find it offensive or old-fashioned to actually wake up with her head on my chest, my arms encircling her small, pale frame.

But not me. This engrained and innate need to protect and watch over her was buried deep in my heart and soul. I wanted to spend every waking minute with her. I wanted to drive her to work and then pick her up when she was done with her shift, greeting her with a kiss as she got on my bike. I wanted to drive her home to a place we shared together and spend the night worshipping her perfect body until she was screaming out my name over and over. But that just wasn't the kind of relationship we had.

Instead, I would text her, she would text back, and I would take that as an open invitation that she wanted me, even if it was just for the night. My heart raced and my body saluted to attention when she'd tell me to come over. I definitely didn't have to be told twice when she gave me an open invitation. So on nights like these, when she let me adore her and explore her every inch before falling asleep, I assumed she only wanted sex.

And that - I could live with.

But just for now.

There was a pink light beginning to creep over the horizon as I rode my bike toward my apartment, ready to sleep the day away. It killed me to leave Talia sleeping, it really did. One day I'd stay all night and see what she thought - test those boundaries - but for now, I'd give her space.

I had often thought - maybe it was me who wanted it this way? No commitment, get what I wanted and give her what she needed - and then leave, move on with my day, my week, my month. I wasn't sure. I was so fucked up inside, it was hard to decipher what I wanted or needed anymore. All I knew for sure was that I needed a job and something to focus on before I went utterly motherfucking insane.

I pulled into the parking lot of my apartment complex and hurried to my door, anxious for my own bed. After stripping and showering under some hot, steamy water, I fell into bed wearing nothing at all, letting my thoughts of Talia consume me. Lord knows visions of her beautiful face and body was so much better than the ones of sand, smoke, and sordid danger that usually plagued me.

My eyes fluttered closed and blackness took me, but it was anything but blessed or peaceful.

The truck is on its side and I slam my eyes open, wondering just what the hell is going on. One minute I'm driving through the desert with my fellow Marines on our way to check out a possible enemy camp, the next, the truck I'm in is on its side, smoke billowing from the top of it. Groans and moans of pain echo around me. My rifle is still in my right hand, but I cannot move my left. It's stuck between my seatbelt and the butt of the rifle.

I yank hard to free myself, my brain still in a dazed fog as to what the fuck just happened. I manage to free myself by cutting the seatbelt off with my knife and crawl from the vehicle. About 20 feet away, I see a man lying on the ground. He's writhing around in pain, so I stagger to my feet, coughing from the smoke, and go to him.

Kneeling down, I set down my weapon and my eyes take him in. He's big guy, dark hair, muscular. As my gaze scans his body for injuries, my eyes bulge at the hulking piece of shrapnel sticking out from his leg. His camouflage pants are shredded, the blood beginning to bloom around the wound like a fast-moving storm overtaking a countryside. The guy is grunting and trying not to scream, the vein in his neck bulging fierce while his face turns purple.

"Get this damn thing out of my leg right fucking now!" he screams at me in a painful desperation.

I lick my lips and take a shuddering breath. I really want to pull it out of his leg. My God, it looks like it hurts more than anything on Earth. But my basic first-aid training kicks in, and one of the most important rules was – 'never remove an impaling object.' I knew his femoral artery had to be pretty damn close to the wound, and that piece of metal could be the only thing keeping his artery from spouting a fountain of blood and killing him in less than 15 minutes.

I could kill him if I pulled that fucker out.

Sgt. Hawthorne is what his uniform reads. I didn't know him at all before this roadside bomb had rocked all our worlds, and this was a hell of a way to meet someone.

"Get the fucking doc now!" I yell to my comrades, trying to show this guy that I was desperate to help.

I could tell he was trying to be strong but I definitely

did not think anyone with this kind of wound could last very long. He's going to pass out from the pain or continue screaming. Or worse – die. I should probably check him for other injuries. What if the shrapnel hit him elsewhere?

His head is thrust backwards and he's got his eyes closed. He was a tough fucking bastard and I had to respect him for that. My eyes begin to scan him for other wounds, and with my right hand squeezing his thigh, I try to keep the pain at bay. I then lift my left hand to shove up his shirt. There's so much blood everywhere, I have no idea what is splatter or what could be new wounds.

I look down at my hand and something doesn't look right. Why are my pinky finger and ring finger shredded? They look like hamburger and are bleeding everywhere. Why doesn't that hurt? Shouldn't that hurt?

The clink of the smoke marker hitting the ground and a smudge of blue smoke rising in the air faintly registers as the screams of other Marines around me resonates in my ears. I rip a piece of my shirt off and wrap it around my hand so I can help Sgt. Hawthorne here while we wait for the chopper, which I can hear pulsing closer and closer. I'll deal with these injuries later. Probably just a couple broken bones or cuts…

I gasped out loud as my eyes slammed open. I. Hate. That. Fucking. Nightmare.

I cradled the sides of my head in my hands. *Make it stop.*

I didn't get very much sleep after the nightmare that never left me alone, and I knew sleep was futile. It was early afternoon now, and decided I should probably go see my mother.

Knowing she'd grill me about what I was doing with my life, if I had a girlfriend, if was ever going to settle down, and anything else she felt like throwing at me, I decided to spare myself the hassle and just call her instead. I could get the third degree over the phone instead of in person, and not waste any gas or miles on my bike doing it.

I flipped the covers off and pulled on some athletic shorts that were on my floor. Yawning, I raked fingers through my hair and wandered into the kitchen. I tossed a few scoops of ground coffee into a filter and hit the start button.

Scrolling through my phone while it brewed, the pungent aroma of the coffee hit my senses and immediately reminded me of Talia. She always smelled perfectly pure and amazing, but there was also that faint smell of coffee that lingered on her because of her job. I smiled a little as I shoved the coffee cup under the spitting stream and filled my mug. Sipping it carefully, I decided I needed to see her again. Today. Tonight. Sometime soon.

I found her name in my texts and shot off one to

her. It's time we had a real date. Fuck all these dumb-ass rules.

After texting her, I called my mom and had a stilted conversation with her about the things I knew she'd grill me about. Did I have a job? Not yet. Did I have a girlfriend? That's a loaded question to which I had no answer except "I'm working on it." And the last - when the hell was I gonna grow up? I shook my head at the last one. If she knew half of the shit I'd seen, she'd gain a shitload more respect for me.

Talia

Ellis wasn't there when I woke up this morning. Did I expect anything different? No. Was I hoping for a small miracle? Yes.

Why did he feel the need to leave when I just wanted him to stay? Had I ever told him I wanted him to stay? Not sure. Maybe it was time I communicated more. But what if he liked it this way? This casual, no-strings-attached hook-up… I liked it, and I hated it.

I laughed to myself. Of course he likes it this way. He's a dude. I'm just a dumb girl who thinks I deserve more when I know I don't.

Nobody wants you, Talia. You're pale, have red hair, and are too shy. Good luck finding a man. Nobody wants an ugly girl. You should wear more makeup.

I shook my head at the negative thoughts that plagued me constantly. The ones my stepfather would pound into me as a young teen. The only escape I had during those early, horrid days was the promise of sneaking out of my bedroom window at night after my parents were asleep to go hang with my friends. Smoke weed, cigarettes, and whatever else my friends could get their hands on.

My mom had no money. She worked in a fancy restaurant waitressing her ass off, and probably flirting with the boss. It was the only way I figured he managed to let her use his address to get me into a school that was halfway decent. Lord knows the school I was zoned for was nothing like the one I actually ended up attending.

Still, I never asked questions. All my newfound friends at the high school, with their designer clothes and fancy makeup and expensive shoes had accepted me. When questioned once or twice at my choice at cheap fashion, I had made up some bullshit about how I hated my stepdad and was rebelling against him with cheap clothes from the second-hand store. The reality was, I only got something new when my mom had gotten some good tips.

The lie about my stepfather hadn't entirely been a lie. I did hate his ugly ass. He was an abusive drunk, slapping my mother around when he was really wasted. He would say hideous things to me after she'd pass out from either drinking too much of the cheap booze he'd brought home for her, or after he'd rough her up some more.

I would lock my door and pray he didn't try to break the lock and come in to scream at me some more. I had put a poster of my favorite band over the fist-sized hole he'd left in my wall one night when he'd rifled through my nightstand and found my journal. The place where I had told my deepest, darkest secrets, thoughts about how I hated him and wished my mom would leave him.

Rick was his name. I loathed him for what he had done to me and my mom. Rick had eventually caused the demise of my mother, feeding her addictive personality with drugs and alcohol until her small, pale frame couldn't take the abuse anymore, and she'd succumbed to an overdose.

I went through bouts of being angry at mom for not being strong enough to stand up to Rick, to a deep, dark sorrow at her gullibility and sensitive nature that had caused her to stay. "He's sick," she'd say, referring to his alcoholism. "I vowed to stay through sickness and in health, and he's sick, Talia," she'd croon, brushing a stray curl from my face, smiling at me with the warm caramel colored eyes that were so much like mine.

Not that I had an argument for that. I didn't actually want to argue, but I was still angry to an extent. Angry at her, angry at Rick, angry at myself. But that was all in the past.

Was I ready to take on a damaged man, just like my mother had? It had ultimately been her downfall. That was not a future I wanted for myself. I was in school, and Bo was there, cheerleading, telling me I was almost done.

The coke, the heroin, the marijuana, the spice… I had tried it all and I had pulled myself out of the mire of addiction. I wasn't going to turn out like her. I wasn't going to let a man tell me what to do, how much money I could spend, where to work or not work, and what kind of person to be. I was going to be my own person.

My phone chirped and I pulled it from my nightstand to look at it. I first noticed the time - 1:42 p.m. Smiling at how lazy I'd been to sleep in this late, I then looked at the text.

Ellis: *I want to see you tonight. Feel like being seen in public with me, sweetheart?*

I sighed. My night was wide open and the thought of seeing him exhilarated me a little, but also scared me.

Yes, he'd been gone this morning when I woke briefly, and my heart ached at the thought of seeing him. I bit my lip in contemplation. He said he wanted to take me out. That, I could do. So was I ready to go out with him instead of just letting him into my bed? Yes, I was. He had my heart, there was nothing mysterious about that.

Well, I think I was. I chewed my cherry-red lip and hit reply: *Yes. What time are you picking me up? PS – I hate Thai food, so just don't.*

I grinned at my sass and hit send. Throwing my phone back on my nightstand, I giggled like a schoolgirl and threw my arm over my eyes.

Chapter 6

Ellis

I punched the air in triumph. She agreed to go out with me. Like, out in public. I was cautiously happy. My brain questioned as to why she hadn't agreed to this before. Then a thought hit me: Had I ever asked?

Meeting her in that coffee shop six months ago had been the best thing to ever happen to me (even above being *sentenced* to becoming a Marine instead of an inmate, as if that was some sort of punishment), and when we first started talking, nothing made me happier than to get a call or text from her. Sometimes, if I didn't hear from her for a day or two, I'd visit her coffee shop under the pretense of just wanting coffee. Sure, I lived off the shit to keep me from dozing off mid-day from the lack of sleep I got at night, but seeing her there in her green apron and wild red hair was more of a buzz than any caffeine jolt could ever be. But I think she knew it, too. She would smile shyly while asking what kind of drink she could make for me.

We went on a couple of dates here and there, but after a few weeks, it seemed to morph into just sex. Not complaining about that since it was completely fucking incredible, but knowing what little I knew about women, I knew she probably wanted more than that. But who was I to decide what she wanted? I was only in charge of my own self - what I wanted, what I needed, what I craved, and what I had to have. Talia was all those things. Did she feel the same? I thought so.

I chuckled at myself. These thoughts were starting to sound way too chickish. What the fuck was wrong with me? I should just be happy I had some hot girl willing to let me into her bed.

Blowing out a breath, I silently cursed myself for wishing my brain worked that way. It didn't, but that didn't stop me from keeping up the ruse that it did. While I was happy she had agreed to go out with me, I had to whip down these over-analyzing thoughts and hopes. I was behaving like a stupid, pussy-whipped bastard, and that just wasn't me. I was a badass with tons of skill and no need for something permanent or - *shudder* - emotional. Chicks were just baggage and a hassle that I just didn't need. Right? That's what I kept telling myself.

After fucking off all day looking at job websites and scrolling through social media to see what else everyone else was doing, I got myself cleaned up and put on a fitted white T-shirt with a collared white and blue plaid button-up shirt thrown over it that my mom had gotten for me one Christmas. I left it open down the front. My jeans slid on nicely, and after a squirt of cologne, I plucked my keys from the dining room table and drove my rumbling baby to Talia's apartment.

She opened the door looking irresistible. I had to flog back my desire when my eyes raked over the loose black dress paired with a set of rough worn cowboy boots. Her red hair was wild around her shoulders, eyes twinkling at me in amusement when she caught me ogling her.

Quickly reining in my desire, I smiled coolly and held my hand out. "Ready?"

Talia nodded and bit her lip. "Yep."

I led her to the car, opened the passenger door, and made sure she was seated before I closed it. I smiled and exhaled. I could do this. Why was I so nervous?

The drive to the restaurant was mostly quiet, except when she asked me where we were going. I decided to keep her guessing so I told her it was a surprise. I shot her a sideways glance, trying to gauge her reaction, but it was too hard to unravel. Did she like surprises, or hate them? She was such a closed book, it made me crazy.

I saw her smile as we pulled up outside a brightly and colorfully lit popular barbeque place. There were people standing outside waiting for tables, some smoking, others holding to-go containers, hugging their loved ones goodbye before departing to their respective cars.

Talia opened the car door and got out before I had a chance to open it for her. I went around quickly to her side, and before she could close it, I grabbed her arm and scooted her over so I could close the door myself. She looked up at me in surprise and I fixed her with a serious stare, boxing her in against the car with both arms.

"Do not open the door when you're in the passenger seat. You wait until I come around and do it for you. Understood?"

I said it way more confidently than I felt. I sort of wanted to laugh, but I was also testing her.

Her eyes narrowed at me and once again she caught her lip between her teeth before she said, "I appreciate your chivalry but I really can open my own door."

Surprised and secretly turned on by her confident sass, I said, "Sweetheart, next time I'll lock the doors. Only I get to open and close the door for you."

Nodding, she bit back a smile right before I leaned down and surprised her with a kiss on her beautiful mouth. She gasped right before our lips connected and I smiled against them.

Putting my right hand out, I led her through the crowd and to the hostess station, where I informed the pretty lady behind the podium that I had a reservation. We weaved our way through a throng of crowded tables to a small one for two in the corner. I thanked the hostess, and then we sat down across from each other.

Talia picked up her menu and smiled at me, and it made my chest constrict a little. She was so damn beautiful. "I love this place. I don't get to go out very often so this is a treat. I love barbeque."

I was happy I'd made her happy. I was also sad, and honestly, sort of ashamed I didn't take her out more often. Of course she didn't get out much. College student working in a coffee shop. I doubted she had much spending money.

"So tell me, what's good here?" I asked as her pretty face made serious business of searching the menu.

"Ooh! Fried pickles, I definitely want some of those. And the pulled pork is really good here, too. I think they make their barbeque sauce from scratch…"

She began to prattle on about the food but my eyes had caught a guy two tables over looking at Talia. He had really short light hair, almost blond, and looked to be about my age. He wasn't smiling at her, but just staring at her - and I didn't like it. I didn't like it one bit. While he wasn't exactly looking at her like he wanted to fuck her, he was staring too long. That was enough to make my blood pressure go up.

"I asked you a question," Talia said, her high-pitched voice breaking me out of the death stare I was giving this other guy. Her lips were set in a firm, grim line, clearly annoyed.

Slowly sliding my blue eyes back to her, I said, "Huh? Sorry, what was the question?" I tried to throw her a sincere smile.

Her ginger eyebrows dipped together thoughtfully before she answered, "I asked if you'd eaten here before."

I nodded. "Yes, I love this place. I've lived in Tampa my whole life - well except when I was in the service - and this is one of the best in the city."

Her lips twitched in amusement as she set the plastic-laminated menu down. "Take all your girlfriends here then?"

I wanted to laugh but blond douchebag was staring at my girl again. "No." I answered. "Excuse me real fast."

Watching as the guy got up, I was going to follow him when I saw that once he was upright, he had a perfect left leg, but his right was nothing but a titanium rod from the knee down under his shorts. He didn't look at me as he headed toward the men's room. My determination to fold this guy's teeth back with my fist softened when I saw his disability. Still, he had no right to stare at my girl like that. I would think if he knew her, he'd come over and say hi. Or Talia would be looking at him too, or she'd say something.

Still determined to confront him, I followed him to the restroom. I wasn't sure if I was relieved or agitated that we were alone in there. He was already taking care of business at the urinal when I walked in. I washed my hands and waited for him to finish.

He zipped up quickly and came over to the sink and began washing up.

"Hi," he said to me.

I folded my arms over my chest and measured him with a death stare. "Why you eyeballin' my girl?"

His eyes raked down to my tats and then back up to my face. His chin jutted at my right arm where a USMC insignia had been inked to cover the stupid OAB tat I'd gotten as a young dumbass. "You were in the Marine Corps. Who were you with?"

I looked down at my arm in surprise but tried to keep a neutral gaze. "Why do you care?"

He rolled up the sleeve of his shirt to show me a large USMC tattoo on his left shoulder. "I was Golf 2/8, with two tours in Trashcanistan until this happened." He moved his gaze to the titanium rod holding him up.

I nodded. "Look, I'm sorry about your leg, and

that you had to sacrifice it for a thankless shithole of a country. Bravo 1/7 was who I was with. Twenty-Nine Palms, eight years. Now answer my question, man."

My posture was still defensive, but I wasn't budging. I did soften on the inside to meet a fellow Marine who'd lost so much but my anger was failing to calm past percolating.

"Look, I'm sorry. She looks so much like my ex-wife, and I've... just been dealing with that for a while. I'll stop. I promise I don't know her."

I nodded. "I'd appreciate it." I turned to leave and he grabbed my arm.

Looking down at his hand around my bicep, my gaze traveled slowly up to meet his green eyes. "You probably should get your hand off of me."

He held his hands up in surrender. "I'm Kyle Adams. I think you could probably benefit from this company." He handed me a business card, which I took reluctantly.

I looked down at it.

Harper Mathis, Owner

Mathis Associates

Helping veterans with job placement and counseling

VFW Approved

There was an email address, website, and phone number underneath.

I looked up at Kyle and held the card up between two fingers. "What makes you think I need this?"

Kyle leaned on the counter, seeming to need to shift his weight off his leg. "What's your name?"

I sniffed and lifted my chin. "Ellis Anderson."

"Well, Anderson, what do you do for a living?"

I swallowed down the shameful pride that engulfed me every time I got asked this and gave my pat answer. "I am still looking for work after being released from the Marine Corps."

He smiled slightly, and the handsome bastard looked almost smug. He pushed off the counter and tossed a paper towel into a nearby trash can. As he passed me, he clapped me on the shoulder. "Call Harper. She can help. And thank you for your service, Ellis Anderson."

As he exited the bathroom, he left me feeling like the douchebag I had taken him for not five minutes ago.

Dinner was perfect after that. Talia hadn't questioned why I'd spent so long in the men's room, but she did lift a questioning eyebrow at me briefly once I returned to the table. I'd just thrown her a cocky grin and the rest of the night went smoothly. Kyle never returned to his table, and admittedly, I was partially relieved. I'd felt bad Talia looked like his ex, but I still had to admit I was proud of myself for standing up for my girl. I should have done it in front of her, though. Maybe one day I'd tell her what had happened.

As we got in the car, it seemed to steer itself toward the water, wanting to park on one of the many piers that overlooked the beautiful gulf waters.

Chapter 7
Talia

If I said Ellis had been acting strange during dinner, that really wouldn't be a very factual statement, considering I really wasn't sure what his "normal" looked like. I knew his charms and the way his smile made me melt, and I knew his anger when something random (and usually strange) would cause a reaction out of him, but during dinner, he just seemed… I don't know… stoic?

I'm not even sure if that's the right word. He didn't seem to have been paying attention to me as we were talking about what to eat, then he disappeared to the bathroom for a while. I never asked why he was gone so long, and I didn't want to know, really. That was his business. Hopefully he wasn't in there calling or texting some other girl.

And there it was. My insecurities rearing their ugly head. I didn't think they'd ever go away, but then again, whose ever did?

I sat pondering these things in the passenger seat of Ellis's loud, obnoxious car. Occasionally I'd steal sideways glances at his black hair that shined almost blue under a full moon. The firm set of his shadowed jaw gave him the appearance of being deep in thought. The car, which I think was some sort of domestic thing, Dodge or Chevy maybe – well it was much too loud to listen to the radio, so I just enjoyed its growling purr, grateful it filled the silence between us.

Looking out of the windshield, I could see he had led us to the piers on the western edge of Tampa. The water looked beautiful and peaceful under the bright moon, and when Ellis finally stopped the car and killed the engine, my ears rang a little at the absolute silence.

He left the keys in the ignition and put his hands in his lap, shifting his upper body to look over at me. He was just staring, half of his face bathed blue from the moonlight. The night was warm so he rolled down his window, and I did the same. Once my concentration was away from the window and its breathtaking view, I turned to look at him once again. He seemed like he wanted to say something but was holding back. The glass of wine I'd had at dinner was still buzzing through me, so with more courage than usual, I said, "What's on your mind, Ellis?"

He smiled a little and looked down at his hands, lifting one shoulder in a slight shrug. "Do you think I'm damaged?"

The question took me off guard, as it seemed to be such a deviation from his usual cocky, confident self. Did this mean he felt comfortable enough to open up to me? A tiny spark of hope blossomed in my chest. About the question, though, I didn't believe I knew him well enough to have the answer. But instead of that coming out of my mouth, I grinned a little and reached over to touch his hand, glancing briefly at the missing finger on his left. "Who told you you're damaged?" I was desperate to see a little more into his world.

He shook his head. "Nobody. I just sometimes think I'm fucked up beyond repair."

I cocked my head to the side, my thumb running gently over the top of his hand, understanding he was talking about emotional damage. "Why do think that? Because of being in the Marines?"

"Nah," he said, smiling sadly. "The Marines was the best thing to ever happen to me."

"Then what?" I urged.

He took a deep breath. "Before I joined the military, I wasn't a good person, T. I was involved in some bad shit. Some really bad shit. Shit you don't want to know about."

This surprised me, and saddened me. It made me think of Rick, and I hoped that Ellis wouldn't turn out to be an abusive prick. But instead of voicing that, I just stayed silent, nodding for him to continue, enjoying the feel of the hot night air blowing in through the open windows. The crash of the waves against the pier was a calming sound –

almost cleansing - and I wondered if Ellis felt it, too.

"I can't believe I'm telling you this, but I was sort of in a gang before I joined the Marines." He shook his head and chuckled nervously.

Both my eyebrows hit my hairline and my finger momentarily stopped stroking his hand. "What?"

"Fuck," he murmured. "I shouldn't have told you that."

I shook my head. "No, it's okay, really. Please continue. Tell me what happened."

But he didn't. When he leaned over and fisted a handful of my hair at the back of my head and forced his lips on mine, I figured the conversation was over. The small twinge of disappointment I'd felt was quickly overtaken by the happiness that engulfed me at him opening up to me, even if it was short-lived.

Six months. All this time of him coming over, adoring my body, giving me the occasional small talk, a tiny peek into his past, into his life - and now this. This was huge, and I wondered what had caused him to want to open up like that. I tried to not dwell on *what* he'd told me, though.

I couldn't analyze it any longer when his hand slid up my bare thigh and came to rest just inches from my most intimate spot. His kiss was doing things that nobody had ever done to me before. I lost all thoughts of the over-analyzation of who and what Ellis Anderson was and my raging hormones took over, wanting nothing more than to feel him rocking in and out of me. To wrap my legs around his thick, muscular body and press every inch of my naked form into him. To claim his mouth with mine until he screamed my name into it while I made him forget his own.

His fingers climbed higher up my thigh, finally pushing aside my panties. One eager finger slid into me, slick and easy. I groaned into his mouth. It was him making me forget my own name now.

"I want you, T. I can either take you in the backseat or we can head to my place. Your choice, sweetheart."

It was difficult but I really didn't want to have car sex like a couple of teenagers. "Take me to a bed, now," I breathed into his ear.

He pulled his hand away from my leg and stuck it in his mouth, smiling as he licked his finger. Then he started up the car and drove a little too fast back to his place.

Ellis

I could barely drive home with her hand on my

zipper and her lips so close to my ear. The car was permeated with the smell of sex and heat. How did Talia do things to me nobody else could?

I steered the car toward my house and decided to throw caution to the humid wind and say, "Stay with me tonight."

It wasn't a question, it was a demand, a plea.

She stopped licking my ear and said, "I don't know."

"Why not?" I shot back, immediately regretting the question. I don't know why I regretted asking it, just that I thought I sounded sorta desperate. But wasn't that what I was?

She shrugged, taking that bottom lip captive again. "I… I don't know. I just shouldn't."

We reached a stoplight and I put the car in park. I reached over and ran my hand over her creamy, pale thigh again. I then reached up under her dress, grazing my fingers over the black lace and my pants shrunk another size. "Please."

She stared at me again, that hostage lip and those indecisive amber eyes that gave her away in every way. I knew I had her.

"Please," I said again.

A green light illuminated her beautiful face and I knew I needed to put the car into motion but I didn't care. There were no other cars around so I just sat there, waiting for her answer.

Finally she smiled a little, nodding her pretty red head. "Okay. I'll stay with you."

I smiled in triumph and put the car into gear, heading to my place.

I had a feeling we weren't going to get much sleep tonight. And that was fucking awesome.

She'd been to my place a few times, but had never stayed the night. What in the hell was wrong with us?

I set the alarm to my beautiful car and led us to the door of my little mobile home I rented in this ridiculous trailer park. Thankfully, this one was one of the "higher end" mobile home parks, the roads paved and lawns manicured, a little kiddie park on its edge with play equipment and a basketball hoop.

Talia didn't seem to care at all. After I locked the door, I threw my keys, phone, and wallet onto my kitchen counter then looked at her. She had a mischievous, wild look on her face, and I slid the purse she had slung around her body off over her head and threw it on my couch. But she didn't move.

Crouching down, I slowly removed one of her boots and set it next to the sofa. I then removed the other, and looked up to see her staring down at me in amusement.

I kissed the tops of her purple painted toes and began trailing kisses up her ankle, knee, then the inside of her perfect thigh. Reaching up while my lips stayed on her skin, I pulled her panties off and tossed them… somewhere.

Standing slowly, I slid my hands up her hips, taking her dress with me. She raised her arms voluntarily when it reached her ribcage, and I tossed the dress off of her with one swift movement.

The black lacy thing holding her breasts in place had to come off. Pressing my body into hers, I kissed her softly on the mouth and then threaded my fingers through the curls on the back of her head. With slow movements that were killing me, I slid my hand down her back and popped the latch on her bra, releasing it as I slid both straps off her shoulders, never breaking the kiss. She groaned into my mouth when I tossed it to the side, then I pulled apart from her for a fraction of a second to lose my shirt.

I pressed my bare chest into hers and pushed her to walk backwards toward my room. The door was already open and we kept walking and kissing until we reached my bed. The backs of her knees hit the mattress and she fell with a giggle, me following.

Talia slid on her back until her beautiful head was on a pillow and I put myself on top of her, leaning down to lick and kiss every inch of her body. My dick was straining unbelievably hard against my jeans, so I yanked them off, tossing them onto the floor. Underwear? No. Who has time for that?

I was on top of her, my cock pressing into her thigh.

"Please, Ellis. I need you. Please," she breathed into my ear.

Oh, hell.

I smiled down at her, my hand pinning her down on her belly, and looked at my nightstand. Knowing it held what I needed, I reached over and pulled out a box. *Fuck! Empty.*

A mild panic began to overtake me. I slid over and began rummaging through the drawer until relief flooded me at the feel of a small, round foil wrapper. I pulled it out. I don't remember buying this brand but who cares. I needed it now.

Note to self: Go buy more Trojans tomorrow.

I ripped it open and slid it on, looking back at my girl, her lip in her teeth again, making me absolutely insane. Did she do that on purpose, that lip biting thing? Or did she even know she was doing it? I didn't care. It made me stand to attention and that's exactly what I needed right now.

Her legs were already open so I positioned myself between them. Looking down at her, she was smiling wickedly up at me. I grabbed both her hands and pinned them above her head, wrapping my hand around her delicate, thin wrists. She gave no resistance at all.

Without breaking eye contact, I plunged into her silky depths, gasping in relief. I kept her hands hostage as I watched her beautiful, naughty expression turn to one of surrender. Her eyes closed and her eyebrows dipped together, her breaths getting faster. I felt her wet muscles clench around me and then she was panting at me to keep going.

I pounded her harder. She smiled, then concentrated again, her hips bucking to meet mine as I continued to thrust as hard as I could.

She made a strange mewling sound and relaxed a little, and so did I. I kept moving, looking down at her as her hands were pinned above her head. My right arm had them captive, but my left hand was free to do… whatever it wanted.

I used the flat of my palm to run it over her peaked nipple, causing her to moan. I then ran it over the plain of her belly, circling my finger around her bellybutton, continuing my thrusts as she met me stroke for stroke.

Pressing my hand down to her beautiful mound, I then slid a finger down to her sensitive nub, circling my finger there as I felt us both moving together, me inside her then out, then in again. Watching the movement was too much as I felt the pleasurable pressure continuing to build inside me.

Then I felt her clench around me again. Her nipples went hard instantly and her hips bucked in time with mine.

"Oh, God, please," she cried out, slamming her hips against mine.

I was completely undone. I felt my eyes roll back as I lost everything I had inside of her.

Then I felt something strange. It almost felt like a pop. All I knew was that the head of my cock was suddenly the only thing I could feel inside of her. It was the most intense, pleasurable feeling ever. Every burst of what I let loose was rushing out of me, and I could feel every minute detail. I'd never felt anything so... fucking awesome.

I collapsed on top of my beautiful girl, my body shaking from the experience, my emotions skittering all over the damn place. That was unlike anything I'd ever felt. It was incredible… indescribable… should I say beautiful?

I pulled out of her and gasped when I went to yank off the condom. The entire tip was ripped and hanging open.

The damn thing had busted open.

Fuck me.

Chapter 8
Talia

I rolled over as soon as he was out of me. *Oh, my God.* Now I knew why I put up with not knowing much about Ellis. His cock was a magic wand and I was under its damn spell.

After pulling out, he'd done something with the condom and came behind me to wrap his body close around mine. His form molded perfectly to me, but he didn't seem perfectly relaxed. He still felt a bit stiff, but maybe that's just how he was. I cursed myself for not knowing him better, but that was short-lived when sleep began to take me. I was exhausted from the day, and as much as I wanted to roll over and stare into his mesmerizing eyes, I just couldn't. My body was a useless heap of spent energy and I needed to sleep a little.

I'd been over to this little mobile home of his before but I'd never spent the night. What was the morning going to be like? It wasn't like he could just take off. He lived here. And I certainly wasn't going to just leave. I'd look into the crystal blue depths of his eyes in the early morning light and hopefully we'd make love again.

But was that what we were doing? Making love?

Or were we just having sex? Two people who were very attracted to each other fulfilling a need in one another? I wasn't sure. All I knew was that from the moment I'd met Ellis Anderson, he'd captured my heart.

I'd been furious with myself the moment I had actually admitted to myself that I had let him have my heart. I'd been lying to myself, saying the physical attraction was just that - someone to have fun with. But then every time we slept together, I realized I was chipping off a small part of my heart and soul a little more to him each time.

How the hell did people have "casual sex"? Because I most certainly wasn't cut out for it. So why was I doing it? At first I didn't know. All I knew was that when he was in my presence, I couldn't say no to him. What did that make me? Some sort of whooped little girl?

I wasn't sure. And it frustrated me that the lines were blurred so badly. I had wanted a definition to what we were. Boyfriend and girlfriend? Booty-call only? Future exes? I was going insane…

If I was just his "booty call" he wouldn't take me out in public, right? He'd keep me on speed-dial and ask to come over when the need arose. That's what it seemed like at first, and with me dealing with the death of my mother, the busyness of school, and my job, I sort of didn't care. But now - six months into it - I should care, right?

I did care. I hated to admit it, but I did.

These thoughts were making me crazy. I drifted off to sleep with Ellis's perfect body spooning me and told myself to stop overanalyzing shit and just enjoy him.

I sure hoped my heart would obey my mind one of these days.

When my eyes fluttered open the next morning, the confusion was replaced with annoyance. I was in Ellis's bedroom, but I was alone.

Ellis was gone.

I threw back the covers and got up, stretched, and found his shirt on the floor. Shoving it over my head, I used his bathroom then wandered out into his living room. The whole entire mobile home was utterly quiet, I could practically hear crickets. Except it wasn't night. Sun was streaming in through every window, and making my way to one of them, I could see his car in the same spot he'd left it the night before. Before he'd made love to me in his bed - more than once.

Although when I searched the entire home, Ellis was nowhere to be found. I unlocked and opened the back door, and with both arms wrapped around me, wandered out to what could be considered a backyard. It was nothing more than some patio furniture and a little grass, but he was nowhere.

I breathed in deep, gazing at the small park with the play equipment for kids off in the distance. It was vacant but I was sure later on, it would be full of kids.

Wandering back inside, I went into the kitchen and saw the clock on the microwave reading 8:22 a.m. Where the hell was my man?

I saw a coffee pot, and it was full. Pressing the flat of my hand to its glass body, I could feel the heat radiating there. I rummaged through the cabinets until I found a coffee mug and poured some into it. There was a small bottle of vanilla creamer in his fridge and I poured a little in to counteract the bitterness I knew the coffee would assault my tongue with.

I scrunched my nose as the coffee slid down my throat. It wasn't the worst I'd tasted but I could definitely say I was officially a coffee snob. I took a few more sips and dumped the rest down the drain, rinsing out the cup and leaving it in the sink.

How could he just leave me here in his place? The urge to snoop around was overwhelming, but I just couldn't. Would I want him nosing around my place as I slept or if I'd left?

I laughed at that. I'd never leave him asleep in my own damn bed. Fuck him for doing that to me. Maybe I *should* snoop around.

Sighing at my own morality, I shook my head and found my dress and purse strewn over the couch. I tossed Ellis's shirt off and put on the bra, panties, dress, and purse, and smiled when I found my keys at the bottom of my purse. Then I cursed when I remembered my car was at my apartment, and I was trapped here.

Damn.

Pulling out my phone, I didn't see any messages from Ellis. No text, no note, no nothing. I began to type furiously with my thumbs.

I don't know where you are, but you need to get your ass back to your house. I need to get home.

I made no effort at being nice, courteous, or flirty. The longer I sat here, the more pissed off I got when I didn't get a reply. After about an hour, I gave up hope that he had just left to go out and breakfast or something. I was so out of here. I picked up my phone and searched through the contacts, hitting send when I located the one I wanted.

Chapter 9

Ellis

The motorcycle's roar soothed my ears and relaxed me, then the vibration of my phone in my pocket made me stress up again. I knew it was her. She was texting me, asking where the hell I was. But I didn't have an answer for her. I was everywhere and nowhere, driving down the interstate with no destination at all. And I didn't care. I had to clear my head. I'd worn no helmet because I didn't care about the law right now. I guess it was in my nature not to care. I'd practically started my life off as a criminal, hadn't I?

Woman in love with an ex-con, gets pregnant by him, then has me… never met my dad 'cause he ended up back behind bars, now serving a 25 year federal sentence for a drug crime and mom refused to bring me to a prison visiting room to see him. And did I care? Not really. Probably why I'd taken the path I'd taken. Drugs, guns, gang-banging. It was in my nature. It was what was comfortable to me. I shouldn't be proud of that - and I wasn't. The Marine Corps had shown me a whole different point of view. A side where you saved lives for no other reason than it was the right thing to do - not take lives because it served your selfish cause. As much of an adjustment that that had been for me, I had learned fast. A drill sergeant barking and spitting in my face about what a lowlife piece of shit I was didn't faze me one bit. I already knew I was a lowlife piece of shit. What did faze me, though, was being sent 5,000 miles away, to the other side of the world, to defend and protect the freedoms of a country I knew didn't give two fucks about me, the United States, or anything else good.

Still, I did what I was told. I loaded and cleaned and assembled and disassembled my weapon like they told me to. I slept and didn't sleep when they'd told me to. I wore what and when they told me to wear. I never asked why. I never complained. The thought of prison and being forced back into a white supremacist gang kept my nose to the fucking grindstone. I wanted no part of any of that.

Do your four years, then you're done.

You're free.

You can do whatever you want.

Stay out of trouble.

Until one day, trouble found me. Well me, and my entire company.

Sent out to scout a possible enemy camp, three other Marines and I took the Humvee out to investigate why the scout hadn't returned. It wasn't the first time we'd been tasked with this, and it wouldn't be the last. So with familiarity, we set off, sure we'd find nothing. But it wasn't what we found, but instead what found us that changed something inside of me.

Like I always did, I thought about that day Duke had almost lost his leg due that that deadly IED. The day I'd almost lost two fingers, but still ended up sacrificing one. I looked down at the place where I should have a pinky finger and the deep scarring of the finger next to it, when a honk from a car behind me caught my attention and burst me out of my military musings.

With both feet planted on the hot asphalt on either side of my bike seat, I looked up to see the light had turned green. *I have got to stop daydreaming at stoplights.*

I wasn't sure where I was going, but I knew that when I'd woken up with Talia this morning, I'd been both happy and scared shitless. I just needed to take a ride to clear my head. I should have left her a note or a text or something, but I was obviously an inconsiderate asshole like that. She'd figure it out, I'm sure.

My bike took me back to the bridge leading over the gulf waters, as it had so many times. This was a familiar mainstay to me, obviously something that helped soothe whatever was scrambling my mind at the moment. And right now, it was Talia.

What had freaked me out so badly about waking up next to her? Wasn't that what I always wanted?

Maybe she didn't though. Maybe I had coerced her into staying. Although I didn't hear her asking me to take her home after she'd collapsed in my arms.

Then there was the broken condom. That had never happened before, and that's probably the reason for my freakout. My stomach was in knots but I wasn't sure if I should tell her or not. I was just going to assume she's on some sort of birth control. I didn't think she had some freaky disease and I know I didn't. I hadn't been with anyone but her in the past 6 months. I tried to calm my brain by looking at the early morning sun glistening over the choppy water. I kept moving and got to the pier I'd been at last night - we'd been at last night - and killed the engine.

My phone buzzed in my pocket again so I pulled it out. Two texts from Talia asking where I was and when I was coming back. I sighed heavily and texted her back:

Sorry, I had to clear my head. I'll be back in 15. Then I'll take you to breakfast.

I pocketed the phone and felt something. I pulled it out to see the business card from that guy Kyle last night. I sat on my bike, my legs out in front of me propping the bike up as I stared at the card. Flipping it over and over in my fingers, I looked out over the water again. I hadn't even given a second thought to the card until today. Maybe I should stop being so complacent and try to get a legit job. I mean, I'm only 25. I'm done with the service and it'll be a long road ahead working shitty jobs and living paycheck to paycheck if I didn't find a career soon. Maybe they could show me where to look for something I'd love to do. I just had no idea what the hell that would be.

As far as the counseling aspect - no thanks. My head was fucked up but I sorta liked it that way. I just hope Talia wasn't too mad at me for leaving her without saying anything. That was a pretty crappy thing to do. On second thought, maybe I should find out why I'm such a fucked-up dick. I pulled out my phone and saw Talia hadn't responded to my text. I dialed Mathis Associates and made an appointment for later that afternoon.

Talia

"Hi, thanks for coming to get me at this ungodly hour," I said to Bo as I got into her car.

She laughed. "It's not ungodly. Ungodly is 5:52 a.m., which is what time Alyssa woke me up this morning." She laughed, thinking about her daughter. Then she looked at Ellis's empty house. "Trouble in paradise?"

"Paradise, hardly," I snorted. I shook my head and crossed my legs after fastening my seatbelt. "He left. I have no idea where he went."

She put her little car in gear and headed out of his mobile home park and onto the main road.

"Wow, no note or anything, huh? That was… rude."

I found a piece of gum in my purse and shoved it in my mouth. "Yeah. I texted him but got no response."

Just then, my phone buzzed. It was Ellis, so I read the text out loud to Bo.

"Clear his head, really? From what? It's 8 in the morning. Wow…" she said after I'd finished reading it.

I nodded, trying not to let tears form in my eyes. This shouldn't be any surprise to me. It's not like I knew him that well. Maybe this is just how he was.

Once we reached my apartment, Bo dropped me off with a hug and told me she'd see me later. We were both working the closing shift, and I was grateful I'd have the distraction this afternoon.

After closing and locking my front door, I suddenly felt really tired. I set my purse and keys on my dining room table and went into my room and fell sleep, trying to stay the tears that wanted to fall. I felt like such an insecure little girl. Ellis was the one making me feel this way, and I didn't like it at all. Maybe it was time I took a break from him. I drifted off to sleep easily.

My practiced smile was hard to keep plastered on today. Ellis was completely blowing up my phone. I'd been on shift for 3 hours and he'd called 4 times and sent me no less than 10 texts.

Obsessed much?

I thought maybe I should just answer it, telling him I was busy, but I didn't want to. He deserved to twist in the wind a little bit, and it made me smile. At least I had some sort of smile for the customers. I couldn't wait to finish school so I could get a job where I didn't have to be "on" all the time. It was damn exhausting.

"You ok, hon?" Bo asked, coming out from the back office, holding the schedule. It was her handwritten rough draft, the one she made sure all the employees were okay with before she put it in the computer. We could log in from anywhere and check our schedule any time of the day or night once it was done. She was such a good boss.

I looked it over, nodded my approval, and thanked her, and took the next order. I was just jumpy today and for some reason, really, really wanted to go get high. I was ashamed to be thinking that way, but just the thought of snorting a couple lines of coke and not dealing with reality for a few hours just seemed so appealing. Old habits die hard.

You're not that person anymore. *I know.*

What would your mom say? *Nothing, she's dead.*

What would Ellis think? *Who cares? Asshole.*

Bo would be so disappointed. *Shut up.*

Nobody had to know. I knew exactly where I could score some, too. I knew where all the good dealers were. I didn't even have to go into a bad part of town to get some. A girl named Ariel at school dealt, and everyone who has ever lived in that world knew it, too. She was making a killing, helping students pull all-nighters with a large choice of coke, meth, or anything else they wanted. Weed seemed to be the most popular, but I was never a fan of that shit. Just made me hungry and sleepy, and really, I was already those things most of the time anyway.

Which is why I'd love to get some coke. Just a little. I wouldn't get addicted again, I would be okay.

Feeling increasingly twitchy, I kept checking the clock, and finally, it was time to close and go home. Getting in my car, I started it and pulled my phone out, scrolling through the contacts until I found

Ariel's name. My finger paused over the contact. Call or text?

Neither, a voice in my brain said. *Think about someone other than yourself.*

Like who?

Everyone you love.

But I don't love anyone.

I'm going crazy. That's it, I'm gonna have to be committed for having full-blown conversations with myself.

"Fuck!" I yelled, throwing the phone into the backseat and heading home. But not before stopping by the liquor store first. I won't do any drugs, but I sure as hell could do a few shots of Fireball before I went to sleep tonight.

I heard my phone ringing in the backseat. "Eye of the Tiger" by Survivor was the sound. That was Ellis's ringtone. When was he going to take the hint?

Chapter 10

Ellis

I steered my motorcycle into the parking garage of a huge building downtown. I removed my helmet and smoothed down the dressiest polo shirt I had in my closet. Taking the business card from the pocket of my khakis, I could see I had to take the elevator to the 17th floor. Easy enough.

So why was I so nervous?

The elevator dinged my arrival and got out to immediately see a wall of glass, one door set into it marked "Mathis Associates" in frosted writing. I walked through and a male receptionist greeted me.

"May I help you?"

I nodded. "Yes, I have an appointment with Harper Mathis."

He stood and smiled. "Right this way."

We walked amongst a throng of desks and cubicles until we reached another glass-walled office overlooking the city marked "Harper Mathis, Owner." The receptionist guy knocked lightly. "Your two o'clock is here, Ms. Mathis."

A knockout blonde with eyes the same color as the sky outside her window and wearing her hair in a long ponytail stood up. She was dressed in a sharp black skirt suit and conservative black heels.

She smiled warmly at me, putting out her hand. "Hi, Mr. Anderson. Nice to meet you."

I shook her hand. "You can call me Ellis." I sat in a chair where she indicated.

She took a seat behind her desk and handed me a clipboard. "If you could take just a few minutes to fill that out, then I'll give you my spiel on what we do here."

I took the clipboard and began filling out my name, date of birth, marital and parental status, service branch, dates, regiment, disabilities, and everything else. I listened to her talk while I filled it out.

"So this is my nonprofit business. We help veterans from all branches, who have recently released from the military, re-integrate back into the real world, so to speak. A lot of vets don't need help but some need a little "hand-up" if you know what I'm saying. We don't do hand-outs here, but we do offer job placement and counseling at no charge. We can also refer to you to support groups, if needed, speciality medical professionals, and we always encourage vets to get involved with their local VFW, which is also a very good resource for vets."

Interesting, I thought. Pretty awesome actually. I finished filling out the forms quickly and handed the clipboard back to Harper.

She took a look at it. “Referred by ‘Kyle Something’.” She chuckled. “Kyle Adams? Kind green eyes and a metal rod for a leg?”

I nodded. “That’s him. He’s pretty nosy, too, but I’ll let it slide since he’s a fellow Marine.”

She smiled in genuine at that, her blue eyes sparkling. I noticed no wedding ring, but told myself this was just business and I shouldn’t be flirting. Not only that, I had a huge amount of ass-kissing to do to a certain redhead when I was done here. She didn’t want to answer my calls and texts, then I’d just show up at her house. I thought about going to the coffee shop, but that boss of hers seemed like a real mama bear, and I didn’t want to deal with her at all.

“So, Ellis, I see you indicated that you have disabilities here. Do you want to tell me what they are, or if there are there any restrictions you might have?”

“Physically?” I asked.

She nodded. “Yes, we’ll start with that.”

“Aside from this,” I said, holding up my left hand to show her my missing pinky finger, “I’m as healthy as a horse.” I thought about poor Duke Hawthorne and the limp he now had, and surpressed a shudder.

“Can you shoot a weapon with that?” she asked,

typing into her laptop as I spoke. It didn't seem to have fazed her at all.

"Yes, ma'am. I can shoot a perfect score."

"Awesome. Now, mentally. Any PTSD?"

I nodded and shifted in my seat. "Yeah, so they say, but I'm good. Really. I have a recurring nightmare all the time, but I don't lose a bunch of sleep like some dudes I know." And I felt guilty for that, I really did. Some guys I'd served with were really, really fucked up. I'd seen the same shit they had – bodies burned to a smoky crisp from roadside bombings, beheaded bodies of the enemy left to rot in the sweltering sun, dudes getting shot, helicopter crashes, and everything else. But people handle things differently, and I believed I had some sort of jacked up blackened heart or something, because it didn't affect me like it probably should have. And that scared me sometimes. Probably why I almost became a criminal. I was literally born with no fucks to give. I was just grateful I didn't have that insominia shit like some of my buddies.

She quietly finished inputting my information in the computer, then read the results once it beeped at her.

"You're single, no wife, no kids, no baby mamas, right?"

I smiled and nodded.

"No girlfriend?" she asked, her lips twtiching.

I let out a breath. "That's... complicated."

"I see," she said, nodding her head.

"You interested in law enforcement work? I've got connections in the Tampa P.D. if you're interested. You seem very tough, and I bet you take no crap from anyone. Am I right?"

She probably saw the lack of pain or emotion in my eyes like everyone else did. I stiffened at her question and then asked her one of my own. "Do you wanna know why I joined the Marines, ma'am?"

She smiled and folded her hands together on top of her desk. "Absolutely."

"I was sentenced by a court of law to join. I was in a white surpremecist street gang in Orlando when I was a teen. My choices were either prison or the military after being arrested for a felony. And not just any branch, specifically, the Marines. I obviously chose correctly."

Her eyes went wide, then she regained her composure. "Wow, that's... rare. I don't think I've ever heard of that happening in this century."

I laughed. "So I've heard. I never told anyone I served with. So now just you, my ma, and Judge Perkins knows."

"Interesting. So you're saying you don't want to work in law enforcment?"

"I will say that working as a street cop would probably not be good for me. I know a lot of bad people, and a lot of them have long memories. Probably wouldn't be good for my reputation. No street cred and all that." I winked at her.

She nodded contemplatively. "I see. Any computer skills?"

I laughed. "None at all. I can barely use my smartphone."

She was quiet for a minute. "So how comfortable *are* you around criminals?"

I'd feel right at home! I wanted to tell her, but instead I said, "Criminals don't scare me. I'm sure they'd be more afraid of me than I would be of them."

She grinned. "I have the perfect job for you."

She hit a few buttons on her computer and printed out a job application for the Federal Bureau of Prisons.

Oh, hell.

Talia

I really wasn't surprised to see Ellis sitting on my

doorstep with a bouquet of roses in his hand. He looked ridiculously handsome and I kicked myself for licking my lips. I'd ignored his texts and calls for almost a week straight, and I knew it would eventually come to this.

"What are you doing here, Ellis?" I sighed, moving past him to put my key in the door.

He stood up and wrapped his arms around my waist, the flowers in my face as he leaned down and kissed the back of neck. I shuddered in pleasure and then cursed my body's reaction it always had to his touch. I got the door open but didn't go inside. Instead, I twisted out of his arms and turned around and looked up at him.

"I've missed you," he said, staring at me. I could see the sincerity in his eyes and tried to not let his gaze undo me.

"You hurt me," I blurted out.

He nodded. "I know. I see that now. I'm fucked up, which causes me to fuck up even more. It freaked me out that you spent the night –"

That pissed me off. "You *asked* me to spend the night, Ellis! Practically begged me…"

"I know, I know, which was why I didn't understand why it freaked me out. I've long since stopped trying to analyze why I do the things I do. I just try to learn from them, then roll with it."

"Unbelievable," I muttered under my breath,

turning around and walking into the apartment.

Ellis followed me inside, then closed the door. "I'm sorry, T. I am, it won't happen again. I left you alone for a few days when you stopped responding to me. I wanted to give you space."

When I said nothing to that, he continued. "I want to make it up to you."

He stepped closer to me and handed me the flowers, which I took, but didn't look at. I was mildly excited because no one had ever given me flowers before, but I tried to keep my face neutral. "I don't know..."

"Have you ever been to Universal?" he asked, referring to the big amusement park in Orlando where all the lore of film and TV came to life.

I responded flatly, "Yes, on a field trip once when I was in middle school."

He smiled. "Well I got a pair of passes. We'll go spend the day and then we'll stay the night at the park's hotel. I'll buy you anything you want. I want to start doing things as a couple. Get to know you better. Treat you like a princess."

Trying not to let my mouth hang open in shock, I set the flowers down on the table and then cocked my head to the side, my arms folded across my chest. "Why? Why now, Ellis? I thought you just wanted to sleep with me. I've always wanted more than that, but I never pushed you. You're always so closed off and angry, and I assume you have some issues from being in the military, but I never wanted to rush you into something you obviously didn't want. So why the change now?"

"Because I just want you. Any way I can have you."

He moved in and gently but forcibly removed my arms from their defiant posture and threaded them around his neck. His arms encircled my back and he cradled me up against his hard chest. I didn't give any resistance because obviously, I'm a weak addict and he was my fix. Last week, when I really wanted that coke, I had resisted. And I was proud of myself. Sure, I'd come home and drank a little cinnamon whiskey, but I didn't get high. Hell, I'd barely gotten a buzz.

Now, here I was, faced with a drug of a different kind and I was powerless to even want to say no. I want to say yes, I want to get my fix of his addictive eyes and body, his tongue all over me, his deep voice growling commands in my ear. I wanted it all and I was going to give in.

"Yes, I'll go to Universal with you. But please do not hurt me like that again, Ellis. The rejection was almost unbearable."

He kissed my forehead. "I didn't reject you. I was just a selfish asshole. There's a difference. Please say you'll forgive me."

I nodded and sighed. "I forgive you."

He smiled in triumph.

Too easily? Sure. Just call me Talia the Weak Addict. It fits.

Thankfully, I didn't have to work the next day. Neither did Ellis, and that made me curious. I'd asked him once before where he worked, and he had told me he was still looking for work after leaving the Marines. Knowing a tiny bit about the military from one of my coworkers, I had asked him, "Well, what did you do in the military? What skills did they teach you?"

His reply had been flat. "How to kill people."

Alrighty then. I didn't ask again. I didn't know where he got his money from and I wasn't going to ask. Honestly, it bothered me a little, but was always afraid to say the wrong thing. I'd seen his temper a couple of times and I really didn't want to see it again.

Miraculously, he hadn't stayed the night last night. He'd hinted at it, and even though I had said I'd forgiven him, I really wasn't all that truthful. I was still mad and hurt. So I'd told him I was tired and would see him tomorrow, and aside from a very sensual kiss that almost made me change my mind, he hadn't pushed. That, ironically, sort of turned me on even more that he'd been courteous, respectful, and gentlemanly about my decision and I almost changed my mind and told him to stay.

Stupid female brain. Why does being a girl have to be so damn complicated? I envied the male mind. Simple, uncomplicated, no long inner monologues about feelings and decisions. Just food, sex, and sleep.

Ellis picked me up in his muscle car and we drove the hour and a half from Tampa to Orlando. I was dressed in white capri pants and a dark blue halter top and some comfortable sandals. In my overnight bag, I had clothes for tomorrow, some toiletries, a gigantic bottle of sunscreen, and a big floppy hat. Burning to lobster status was not my idea of a good time. My damned pale skin didn't tan, so I had to protect it well.

The drive was pleasant and when we reached the park, Ellis found a spot that was nowhere near the front. He cursed a little but I didn't mind. I could use the exercise and I had a feeling I'd be getting plenty of it today - and tonight.

We finally made our way to the front entrance of the park. He presented tickets and we waited in line at until we were finally let in. The park was absolutely magical. Even better than I remembered it - not that I had that great of a memory of it.

I was on sensory overload. My eyes darted from a *Men in Black* exhibit to the adorable Minions of *Despicable Me* to the magic of *Harry Potter*. I wanted to do it all and see it all.

And we did.

Every exhibit was captivating. Every ride and tour was perfect. I loved TV and movies and smiled at the memories each of the exhibits brought me. I couldn't believe I had waited this long to visit this park as an adult.

After going on five or six rides, Ellis asked if I was hungry.

"Starving," I said, smiling up at him.

He grinned back. "Come on, I see a little food stand over there."

It hadn't gone unnoticed by me that he hadn't held my hand all day. He'd slung his arm around me a few times, but I was trying not to let it bother me that he didn't want to hold my hand, as stupid as it sounds. So I stood firm, rooted to the spot as I said, "Okay."

He went to walk but then stopped when he realized I wasn't next to him. He turned around and I could see his eyebrows dip in question behind his black sunglasses. I smiled at him behind my Ray-Bans and he walked toward me, coming to stop in front of me.

"Aren't you coming?"

"Aren't you going to hold my hand?"

He hung his head in a dramatic gesture and ran his right hand down his face. He looked down at his left hand and held it up. "It's kinda gross, I know. Wasn't sure you wanted me holding your hand with it."

I looked at the missing pinky finger and the one next to it was pretty scarred up and a little bent out of shape. Why was he acting like I'd never seen that before? It never bothered me when he used it to touch my body.

"I don't care. Why don't you tell me how that happened?"

Quickly, he grabbed my hand and kissed it. "Some other time. Don't wanna talk about it right now. I'm so sorry I didn't hold your hand earlier. See? I'm an asshole…"

I stopped walking again and looked up at him, putting my fingers up to his face. "Look, Ellis, I'm gonna make this easy for you. Everything you've ever heard about girls is true, okay? We want you to hold our hand. We want you to take charge in the bedroom, and even outside the bedroom sometimes. We want compliments, flowers, and to be taken care of. Yes, I can take care of myself, but it's nice when someone relieves me of that duty every once in a while."

A mischievous grin lit up his handsome, tanned

face. "Okay, T. You got it." He kissed my cheek and led me to the food booth, where we ate hamburgers and French fries and drank soda and everything else bad for us.

It was the best day ever.

Chapter 11

Ellis

Best damn day ever. I hope she thought the same. Honestly, I'd scored those tickets from Mathis Associates. The pretty blonde owner gave them to me. She said every veteran who had been brave enough to come into her office and admit the needed a little "hand-up" (versus a "hand-out") deserved a day of rest and relaxation. She'd given me a choice on which park tickets I wanted, and while Disney was the main attraction around here, I had always wanted to see Universal Studios. I'd honestly never been to any of the parks, we were too damn poor growing up to afford any of them, so to say I was more excited than a kid on Christmas was probably a fucking understatement.

It paid off, though. The look on Talia's face was just damn priceless. I could tell she'd had about as much amusement park experience as I'd had. None. Watching her reactions and her beautiful face lighting up at all of the incredible rides and stops was unforgettable. Honestly, I found them incredible, too. Shame on me for having lived here my whole life and not visited. To make matters worse, I had lived in Southern California for a few years while stationed at Twenty-Nine Palms. But to be honest, that horrendous traffic and crowds had been sort of a turnoff. It almost wasn't worth venturing into the big city to see Disneyland and Universal. Now I wish I'd sucked it up with my friends to go just for the experience. We had been offered discounted military tickets but I just didn't want to go. Although I admit it was kinda cool to have experienced this for the first time with Talia.

Back then, I had still been in shock that that was my life. Sentenced to serve my country instead of sitting in a prison cell amongst a group of questionable characters who probably would have fueled my unsavory desires and led me down a path of self-destruction from which I'd probably never have returned. So I had just hung out on the base, not leaving it very often, utilizing my smartphone to access the outside world and keep up with everyone else living their carefree lives while I was chained to the Marines.

That's how I'd felt initially, anyway. Resentment and bitterness that this had been my only choice. Anyone who even thought prison was a choice was a stupid asshole. I thought I'd have more freedom in the military. I'd been barely more than an inmate. They told me what to wear and when. They controlled what I ate and when. They told me where I'd live and to shut the fuck up if I didn't like it. They told me I could love, but that it came with a price. Occasional trips home to see loved ones and then back to work. The old cliché "If the military wanted me to have a family, they would have issued me one" resonated loudly in those days, so I just avoided the whole relationship thing. I'd find a pretty girl at whatever port or stop we'd been at and use her to satisfy my needs, then move on to the next one. It was a sordid life, and back then, I really couldn't have cared less.

And now? I sort of didn't care either. Except one girl had invaded my soul and captured my heart and I wanted to do everything for her.

Shit... was this love?

I glanced over to Talia in the elevator of Universal's adjoining hotel I'd booked last night. She was looking at the stuffed Minion with a smile on her face. The cold, stiff organ in my chest felt warm for a minute. Then it began to beat a little wildly. She must have felt my stare because she looked at me, her warm honey eyes piercing me. She was still smiling a little, but her gaze looked more inquisitive.

"You had fun, didn't you?" I asked, desperate for a positive answer.

She nodded right as the elevator dinged.

We got out and made our way toward our room. Why was I nervous? She seemed nervous, too.

I pulled out the card key and let us into the room. Talia set her handbag on the chair and sat on the bed, still clutching the Minion like she was 10 years old.

"You really like that thing, don't you?" I asked, chuckling.

She nodded and pushed some hair behind her ear. "Yes, I love it. I had a lot of firsts today."

Sitting next to her, I put my thigh flush up against hers and looked into her warm eyes. Deciding to take her hand, I clasped it in mine and asked, "Like what?"

She grinned. "Like everything. Universal, someone buying me flowers - yes I know that was yesterday, but still - and someone taking me on a day date and winning me a stuffed animal. I know it seems immature, but I love this thing so much. I'm gonna put it somewhere special when I get home so it doesn't get ruined."

My lips twisted in amusement. She was so damn cute I couldn't stand it. "You look so happy, remind me to buy you stuff more often."

Her face suddenly went serious, her ginger brows dipping as if in thought. I used my thumb to smooth out those brow wrinkles I didn't like and used my other hand to tip her chin up to meet my eyes. "What's wrong?"

"Did you ever find work? I mean, I don't want to take advantage of you."

I chuckled and leaned down and kissed her cherry-red lips. "Not yet, but I've got prospects.

And ya know what? Nobody's ever taken advantage of me. If I didn't want to do it, I wouldn't. I do things because I want to, not because I feel like I have to. You make me want to buy you things. The look on your face is worth it."

A red stain crept up her cheeks and she grinned at me. "Okay, Ellis. Just don't ever sell yourself short. I can pay for my own things."

I shook my head at her silliness and kissed her again, this time gently removing the silly Minion from her hand and putting it on the bed. Her body reclined back and I pressed myself on top of her, kissing her mouth. I then moved to her ear, then down her neck, grinning to myself as she let out a shiver.

The night was absolutely perfect. We stayed tangled up in each other's arms all night, fucking, then sleeping, then waking up to do it again.

And this time, none of the condoms broke.

Bright yellow sunlight filtered in through the heavy curtains covering the hotel room windows. Look at that. I've got my beautiful girl in my bed and I'm not freaked out. I'm happy as fuck. A stupid shit-eating grin lit up my face and I blinked to make sure she was real.

At that same moment, Talia's eyes fluttered open

and she smiled at me, and then yawned, covering her mouth with the back of her hand.

"Sorry, I must have morning breath," she whispered.

I chuckled and wrapped both arms around her naked body and kissed her forehead. "I doubt that."

Hugging her to me, I was sure she could feel my morning wood. There was no way I wasn't gonna be inside her again before we had to check out of this room. With her face pressed into my chest, she began to kiss me there, while her hand moved my backside and began stroking my lower back, and then my ass with her soft fingers. It was gentle as a feather and it was making me rock-hard.

She continued to kiss my neck and my chest, and then slung one of her long legs over my hips and angled hers just right until my tip was at her entrance. Without any self-control, I shoved myself inside of her and we both moaned at the exquisite sensation. Before I could blink, she had me on my back and was on top of me, killing me slowly with the seductive gyrations of her hips.

My eyes wanted to close but I wouldn't let them. I stared up into her face, those full pouty lips and those eyes the color of coffee with a little cream in it. When her teeth took that bottom lip hostage and she closed her eyes, I just about lost my shit inside of her.

I grunted and closed my own eyes, trying to last. Football. The Gators. They'll beat the Seminoles this year. They'll even beat those Roll Tide motherfuckers. I need to get the oil changed in my car. I should buy Talia a helmet so we can go on coastline bike rides. I need to get online and apply for that job at the prison. Did I want to work in a prison? Might help me expend some of this energy. I wonder if they will teach me how to put on handcuffs? Then I can cuff T to the bed and violate her 10 different ways…

A scream broke me out of my musings and my eyes slammed open to see her head thrown back, her pale skin flushed beet-red and blotchy, her mouth half open in a moan of appreciation. It was then I felt her sweet walls clenching around my hard cock, and I did lose it. I pushed her off of me and made sure I didn't lose it all inside of her. The condom had already broken once. We didn't need to tempt fate a second time.

She had a slight look of shock on her face when her body landed flat on her back, until she realized what I was doing… showering her in all the stickiness I had to offer.

Ironically, we both laughed when I collapsed on the bed.

We were like a couple of 16-year-olds.

After showering, then checking out of the hotel, we went and got lunch at some sushi place. Now, I did not care for sushi, but apparently, Talia loved it, so I just ate it. Because really, when you spend a year eating MREs and sand, you just stop complaining about food and just eat the fucking shit in front of you. Raw fish wasn't something I'd eat voluntarily but I'll admit it wasn't as bad as I thought it would be.

Spending some time walking around the waterfront shops that surrounded that restaurant, we both decided to call it a day. Exhausted from all the excitement of the past couple days, we got into my car and I navigated the streets on my way to the interstate to head back to Tampa.

The last light before the freeway entrance was still red, but I heard a honk from behind me. Talia and I both turned around and saw an angry driver flailing his fists at us, and being that the light was still red, I couldn't figure out why he looked so pissed and why he'd honked. Ignoring the ass (which wasn't easy) I turned back around to wait for the light to turn green, and then heard another honk. I turned around again, throwing both arms up, shrugging my shoulders.

"Learn how to drive, asshole," the driver yelled with his head pushed out of his window.

Immediately, my blood ran cold.

I knew that voice. It had been eight years but that

was a voice that would never, ever leave my memory.

Ripper.

How the hell was he out of prison?

I glanced back once more, unable to control myself. His cold black eyes were still the same, but new tattoos covered his neck, and every single finger of both hands were inked as they gripped the steering wheel. His eyes were piercing what felt like my very soul, and his eyebrows were dipped in intrigue. Our eyes had officially locked and I felt my stomach turn over. As recognition slowly dawned in his eyes, my own had to be as big as saucers.

His surprise turned to fury, and he got out of the car, slamming his door, and marching straight over to my driver's door.

In the span of five seconds, I had a decision to make. Two options - hit the gas, run this light, and get the fuck outta Dodge, or confront the problem head-on.

Since I'm a loose cannon whose brain writes checks his body probably can't cash, I looked over at my beautiful girl and said, "Stay in here, and do not - I repeat - do not get out of the car. Understood?"

Her eyes were wide with fear but she said nothing, just nodded and clutched the stuffed Minion to her chest. My own chest clutched painfully at the fear in her eyes. It probably reflected a little in my own eyes.

I got out of the car and closed my door and met this thug head-on. I threw my sunglasses on so he couldn't see into my soul (though I was sure it was too late for that), and I put my arms out. "What the fuck is your problem? Why are you honking at me?" I decided to go with ignorance for now. Maybe he hadn't recognized me. I intentionally lowered my voice down another octave.

Ripper went to speak and I could tell he was about to go off on me for whatever reason, and he suddenly froze, his face turning from angry to suspicious. His clothes were extremely… urban. Black chino pants cinched at the waist with a belt, the band of his designer underwear showing out of the top, a tight white tank top showing off all his ink, and a black, flat-billed baseball cap with FUCK OFF written in white.

"I know you," he growled out, piercing me with his dark eyes. His skin looked pale next to them and his face really did seem to be turning red. He looked like he'd had a rough few years, too.

Ignoring that, I said, "Why are you harassing me at a stoplight? What's your problem?" It was so hard to keep a straight face. Not that I wanted to laugh. I didn't know what I felt, but I did know I really wanted to get out of there.

"Holy fuck. LT? Is that you?"

Oh, fuck.

How do I answer that? Truth. The only way. "Yeah, that's what I used to be called."

He stepped closer to me. "Where the hell you been?"

Shit. "Here and there, dude."

"Well you're a shitty driver, LT. You cut me off back there..."

"So what, Ripper? Why don't you grow the fuck up and stop harassing people at stoplights?"

He grinned in triumph, but it wasn't friendly. Then he looked at my ink. "Are those fucking military tats?"

"Are we done here?"

He laughed and pulled a small handgun from the waistband of his pants. "No, asswipe, we're not even close to being done. I want to know how I've spent the last seven years fighting to stay alive inside a penitentiary and you've been nowhere to be found. You fucking snitched, didn't you? I knew it." He raised the gun and pointed at me, and then I heard Talia scream.

His head jerked in that direction, and he made his way toward the passenger side of my car. I rushed over to stop him, not caring that he had a gun, but I was too late. He had yanked open the car door and pulled T out by her hair, while she continued to scream.

"Get your fucking hands off her right now or I'm gonna kill you. I swear to God, I will kill you," I ground out, my hands in balls by my sides, considering going for my own .22 I kept under the seat. But what good would that do? Someone would end up shot.

Dammit! How did a chill weekend at an amusement park turn into this?

My past had caught up to me, that's how. *You knew it was gonna happen one of these days,* I reminded myself.

"Ellis," Talia squeaked out in a panic, her eyes dripping tears in streams down her cheeks.

"Shut up, bitch," Ripper said in her ear but looking at me with that cold look in his eyes.

"Don't talk to her, asshole. Let her go now and I won't kill you, you fuckwad. I mean it."

"No!" he raged, spitting into the late afternoon air. "Tell me how the hell you avoided prison and maybe I won't fuck her in the street right here, in front of you and everyone else. You snitched, didn't you?"

"How do you know I didn't do time?" I asked, my eyes not leaving the gun in his hand.

"You stupid fuck, I've got connections at every Florida state prison. Nobody's ever heard of you.

Trust me, I asked."

"Maybe you have shitty connections. You know, criminals aren't exactly the most reliable sources. Just sayin'."

What was wrong with me? I've resorted to making jokes. I must be certifiably insane. Or nervous as hell.

He grinned and his smile made my stomach turn. He looked at Talia and fingered one of her curls. "She sure is pretty. Tell me, LT, do the curtains match the drapes?" He reached down to grab her crotch but she put a knee up to block him and then slammed her head against his nose.

He'd backed away in time so her head didn't quite connect but it was enough of a distraction for me.

I ran over and snatched the gun from his hand, releasing the magazine and expelling the bullet from the chamber in less than two seconds flat as he was stumbling backwards. I'd disarmed this thug in the blink of an eye.

Huh, guess the Marines had taught me something other than how to kill people.

I shoved the handgun's magazine into my pocket and tossed his gun onto the ground and grabbed Talia as she ran into my arms. She was sobbing, and I felt lower than pond scum for putting her in danger. My eyes never left Ripper. He'd fallen backwards onto his ass and was shaking off the shock. But now, suddenly he was getting back up. My body stiffened, ready for a fight.

"Okay, back in the car," I murmured in Talia's ear.

She shook her head and cried, "No. Not again. Please. Let's just go!"

"There's not gonna be a second time," I growled in her ear, keeping my eyes on Ripper, whose own told a story of anger, resentment, and pain. He was about to tear me apart, but it wouldn't be easy. I had enough rage for the both of us and he was going to be a sorry motherfucker if he laid a hand on me. And if he even looked at my girl the wrong way again, I was gonna kill him and then go away for a very long time.

Talia squeaked when Ripper got up and headed toward me. She clambered around to the front of the car. I could swear I could still hear her heavy breathing.

Once he was within arm's reach, I reared my arm back and let my fist fly into his nose. I smiled at the sound of the satisfying crunch my blow had made. He yelled as his nose began to gush blood. Unfortunately for him, that act alone had ignited a fire in me. The blood seeping down his face made me smile with some sort of bloodlust. It was fucking on.

Putting his hand to his mouth, Ripper looked at the blood on his hand and said, "Oh, hell no, you little pussy. I did seven years behind a fence because of you. I'm gonna kill you now, you snitch."

I laughed. Literally laughed. Maniacal, insane, and incredulous. I'd never told on Ripper or anyone else. My trial had been my own and that judge - for whatever reason - had seen something in me he thought could be saved. And he had been right, so very right.

Still, being called a snitch hurt. I knew the code - never tell on your fellow brother. And I hadn't, so to be accused of that infuriated me to code red levels. Pushing him with both hands, he stumbled backwards and I stuck my foot out and tripped him. I watched in amusement as he fell down on his ass onto the pavement.

Immediately on top of him, I got into his face, ripped off my sunglasses, and stared into his dark brown eyes. "Behind a fence, motherfucker? Try spending 8 years in the Marine Corps. I've seen stuff that would make you shit yourself."

I didn't wait for a reply. One final blow to his right cheekbone most likely left it shattered. Did I care? Not one bit. Again, I just didn't have any fucks left to give, and today was no exception.

Thanks, dad. Fucking convict asshole. Sins of the father, passed right down to your only son. One you never cared about.

Hearing sirens in the distance, I ordered my girl into the car and took off onto the highway, staying at the speed limit even though my lead foot wanted to push the car to 100 MPH to expel some of this energy.

I was 25 years old and had been all over the world. I'd been through worse shit. I should be a lot more calm and mature than this, right?

But I wasn't. I was a hot-head. I looked over at Talia and she was sniffling, tears streaming down her face, the little yellow Minion her only comfort.

Because obviously, I couldn't be.

Chapter 12

Talia

What the hell was that back there? Oh, my God. Why didn't he just drive off when that maniac got out of the car?

And "Ripper"? What kind of name is that? I was frightened that Ellis knew the guy – and that the guy knew him! It was clear there were things he hadn't told me about his past. What a real shock. *Not.*

But the fact that thug had mentioned that Ellis should have gone to prison with him had me terrified beyond anything.

I was sad that such a wonderful weekend has been ruined. Couldn't I get lucky, even once, to have someone treat me nice and take me places? I thought I'd had. I thought we'd turned over a new leaf in our relationship – or had just begun to finally build a "real" one. But it looked like that was not gonna happen. It was time for me to put some distance between myself and him. No way am I going to be involved with someone like that. I knew he had a temper but this was unbelievable. Watching him pummel that guy in the street was so awful to watch.

Plus, it's not like I'm going to get over having a gun pulled on me. Not ever. I'll be having nightmares about that for years to come, I'm sure. I looked down at my trembling hands and had to force myself to breathe in and out before I passed out from fear and pain. I tried hard to keep a tear from slipping out of my eye but it was no use. It trailed down my cheek and I wiped it away with the back of my hand.

He pulled up into my apartment complex and I got out before the car had barely stopped.

"T! Wait!" I heard Ellis behind me.

I shook my head, my bag around my shoulder, the Minion under my arm as my voice shook with emotion. "Just go, Ellis. Please. I need some time alone."

He spun me around before I could get the key in the door. I could hear that his car was still running. "No. I'm not going to go. Not like this. Please let's go inside. I need to explain some things to you that I should have told you a long time ago. You deserve to know. I did not mean for my past to collide with my present, and now it's time for me to pay for those sins. But the one price I refuse to pay, though, is losing you. Please."

I turned around and put the key in the door. I opened it, not caring if he followed or not. If he left, fine, I could get some time to think. If he came in and talked to me… whatever. Then I'll tell him to leave once he was done.

"I'm going to turn off the car. Please give me just five minutes, okay?"

I still didn't say anything, I left the door open and went inside.

I heard the car turn off and he walked slowly inside, closing the door behind him. I was standing in the kitchen getting a glass of water. I just glared at him from behind the half-wall counter, my arm propped against the sink.

"Well, speak," I said shakily, not caring if I sounded like a bitch.

He nodded and came to stand on the other side of the counter, sitting in one of the barstools. "T, I was going to talk to you about this when the time was right. This weekend was so damn perfect, I didn't think us talking about our pasts would have been the best thing right now. I just wanted us to be happy and carefree for a couple of days, not bog it down with the heavy stuff."

I nodded, telling him to continue.

He blew out a breath. "When I was a kid, I did not live in a good area. My mom did her best to raise me, but we had no money. My dad was in prison and I was an only child. When I got to high school, I barely attended. I found friends on the street and began hanging out with them more and more. They were not good people, and even though deep down I knew this, I still kept hanging out with them. I learned later through a government shrink that I did this because I needed to feel a sense of belonging from having a broken family unit, and from being left alone so often." He said the last part as if he was quoting from some kind of psych book.

"Go on," I said, still sniffling.

"Well, I ended up in a street gang called the Orlando Aryan Boys." He looked up at me for my reaction. I now remembered him saying something about a gang when we were in the car at the pier but I had sort of blown it off, thinking it was probably just a stupid high school thing. But this really rocked my world.

"An Aryan gang? Really?" I said. "That's really stupid, Ellis."

His face twisted into something between regret and anger. "I know that now. Misguided youth and all that."

"Continue," I sighed.

"So I began to commit petty thefts and other minor crimes like vandalism and stealing parts off of cars and selling them with my… gang. The guy from today, Ripper, he was sort of our leader.

"So, one day we, in our infinite wisdom, decided it would be really cool if we broke into a large department store and stole guns and ammo. We thought it would make us a more powerful gang.

At this point I'd already been shot at twice while entering into another gang's territory, even if it was just a simple restaurant or store that another gang would claim as 'their' part of town. It was all just so dumb." He sighed and raked a hand through his black hair.

"Ripper busted the lock while I tagged the building with *OAB* in spray paint. Again, real smart of us to tell the cops who'd been there, huh? Anyway, the alarms blared and we got away with some weapons and stuff, and I thought we'd gotten away with it 'til some cops showed up at my door with video surveillance photos. I was done. Too many priors and now a felony? I was only 17 and they told Mom they were gonna charge me as an adult, since my birthday was less than six months away."

I was now staring at him in shock, my resolve softening a little. "Ellis, I…"

"Don't, T. Don't look at me like that. I hate that look. I don't do pity or sympathy. Please just let me finish or I just won't…"

I nodded.

"For some reason, the judge had mercy on me. He knew my father was doing time and maybe he saw something in me that I hadn't seen in myself at the time. He gave me a choice. Marine Corps or prison. Believe it or not, at the time, I thought I was such a badass that prison didn't really scare me as badly as it should have. One night when I was in boot camp, I thought back to that day and realized how stupid I was. My mother pretty much didn't even let me choose. I was still a minor and she told me I was joining the Marines and that was the end of that. Or so I thought, until today. Ripper, Mom told me, had been sentenced to 10 years. Guess he got out three years early."

I nodded, knowing more about crimes and criminals than I should. "Probably got paroled early. Overcrowding and all that."

Ellis got up off the barstool and came around into the kitchen. Standing right in front of me, he placed his right arm on the counter, and rolled up his sleeve. He had a large USMC insignia tat that I'd seen plenty of times. He reached down and grabbed my hand.

"Give me one finger," he said.

I obeyed, pointing my first finger at him. He grabbed it and traced a large "O" in the middle of the insignia. Then he traced an "A" next to it, and then a "B."

"I had the OAB tattoo covered with this."

He still had ahold of my hand. I looked really close and could barely make out the covered up letters. If you didn't know they were there, you'd never see them. "Good decision," I said.

He chuckled. "It wasn't my decision. My sergeant

saw it one day while I was coming out of the showers and told me, and I quote, 'You better cover up that fuckin' mess or I'll take a razor blade to it while three other Marines hold you down.'"

My eyes widened. "Wow."

"Yeah I didn't know how to tell him I was still 17 and no tattoo shop would take me, so I sort of avoided the topic. I'd gotten the OAB tat in Ripper's uncle's garage at the time. So anyway, on my 18th birthday, I got this." He pointed to it again.

"I'm not sure what to say," I said, feeling stupid. I was still angry but I was glad I had given him a chance to explain.

"You hate me now?" he asked, rolling his sleeve back down.

I shook my head. "I don't hate you. I'm not one to judge, Ellis." I pulled a beer out of the fridge and handed it to him. I then went around him and sat on the sofa with my water.

"Thank you," he said, sitting next to me.

"I buy those just for you, you know," I said, pointing at the bottle. "I don't drink beer."

He chuckled and popped off the lid. "I wondered." Then he paused as he took a pull from the bottle and then set it on the end-table. "You know, T, I meant what I said that I had planned on telling you all of this. I just didn't want to tell you this weekend. It just felt too perfect to muddle it with ugly truths and stories of my past."

"I know, and I believe you. But isn't that what makes the weekend better? Sharing stuff like this, getting to know each other better? I mean, that's all I've ever wanted since I met you. But you're so closed off all the time, and would only come over for sex, so I took those small moments with you and cherished them because I thought that was all I would ever get."

His eyes were big and he sucked in a breath, then raked fingers through his hair. "God. No. I... I thought the same about you, T. I didn't want to overstay my welcome and all that. Thought you were busy and didn't have time for any sort of relationship, so I also took what you'd give me. And then when you stayed the night last week, it freaked me out. I didn't know why it freaked me out until I forced myself to go on that bike ride and think about it. The only thing I could figure out was that I would actually now be in a relationship, if that's what you wanted. It scared me for about half a second then it made me happy. But you were gone, and pissed, and I thought I'd lost you."

I nodded, debating my next words, but felt it was the right time. "I'm not exactly a golden child either, you know. My past isn't pretty."

He grabbed my hand, and I felt encouraged to keep talking. It wasn't as bad as his, so I hoped he wouldn't judge, but then again, I've seen people break up over lesser things. So it was my turn to bare my soul.

"My mother, she died of a drug overdose. She couldn't deal after my dad walked out on us for his much younger secretary. I had a pretty normal childhood until then but it slowly started to fall apart after that. Mom dated men who were not good, and ended up marrying the worst of them all. Rick was an abusive piece of shit who eventually killed her with all the drugs he fed her. I sat back powerless to watch, finally bolting the day I turned 18. I lived with friends and tried to have my own life, then I got the news of Mom's death, and in a strange twist of fate, I turned to drugs to numb the pain.

"I couldn't hold down a job and would drift from place to place, not caring about myself at all. Then one day, I found out on the same day that not only was I pregnant, but was having a miscarriage. When I began to bleed badly, I passed out and someone took me to the emergency room. You wouldn't believe how painful it is to lose a baby, even one you didn't think you wanted or even knew you were carrying. I hit rock bottom. I felt hopeless, and while I never contemplated suicide, I knew if I kept on that track, I wouldn't live very much longer. I was barely holding onto the job at the coffee shop, so I called Bo to come get me from the hospital. She practically forced me into rehab. The hospital threatened to call the authorities with how much coke was in my system, too. I knew it was time. I went through a painful rehabilitation and got better. Fast forward to now. Been clean two years. Doesn't mean temptation doesn't slither around to entice me back on the wagon every once in a while, though."

Ellis looked at me with the same pity I'd given him. He leaned forward, putting his arms around me and pulling me into a hug. I melted into him and sniffed back tears. It was still so painful to talk about that part of my life. My mom, the shame of becoming an addict, the baby. I avoided it at all costs, mostly. But I felt I owed it to him after what he had told me. Plus I was still emotional and on edge from the day's events. I was a serious mess.

"I'm sorry I'm so messed up. I wish I could change my past, but I can't," I sniffled into his ear.

He murmured back, "We're all a little damaged, T. Some of us just know how to wear our fucked up on the inside and mask it with normalcy on the outside."

That made me smile a little bit. He was so right.

He stood up and offered me his hand and I took it after setting my water down. He led me into the bedroom where he undressed me, and I let him. Then, as I stood there stripped bare, he reached over to the long nightshirt I had laid over the chair and slipped it over my head. Kissing me on the lips, he peeled off his clothes down to his boxers and pulled the covers back on my bed, instructing me to get in. After flipping off the light, he crawled in behind me and pressed his body up against mine. With both arms around me, he whispered, "Goodnight, sweetheart." We both fell asleep quickly. It was nice.

He was there when I woke the next morning.

Chapter 13

Ellis

I woke the next day feeling like a huge weight had been lifted. After I left Talia's, I applied for that prison job, so that was out of the way, and a big relief. I had no idea how long it took to hear back but I wasn't going to stress about it. I laughed at the thought of working in one. I'd feel right at home around those dudes, wouldn't I? Hopefully I got some training on how *not* to feel comfortable around them. And hopefully my past would not catch up with me. The judge had told me since I joined the service and had received an honorable discharge, that my juvenile record would be sealed permanently. I damn near cried hearing that.

Not only did I have that going for me, Talia had forgiven me, she'd opened up to me, too. And damn, I'd felt so shitty when she told me about her past, but the part that hit me the hardest was her miscarriage. My own mother had told me that she had one before my pops had gone to prison. He'd gotten drunk and slapped her around and she lost the baby. She still had a little sonogram picture thing of the baby in her jewelry box. I'd seen it once as a teen when I was going through it to see if she had anything valuable I could hock for some extra cash. I thank God every day all she'd had was cheap costume jewelry crap, because now, there would have been no way I would have forgiven myself for stealing from her. Seeing that baby picture had sobered me up anyway. She had told me about it once but I never asked about it again. Bummer I never had a brother or sister, but they could have turned out even worse than me, and really, the world didn't need that.

After Talia had told me about the baby, I sorta wanted to ask her if she wanted kids ever, but decided not to. I wasn't even sure I did, and it really wasn't relevant. Two fucked up people trying to raise a kid? Probably not a good idea.

I smoothed some goop into my hair and gave myself a quick shave before spraying on some cologne. I again contemplated if I should get a haircut but there wasn't time. Talia was gonna be here in 10 minutes and my house was sort of a mess. I threw on some jeans and a dark blue T-shirt and some button-down thing with a checkered design on it over it. I rolled the sleeves to the elbows and shoved my feet into my Justin boots. I loved these damn boots. Brown, worn, and comfortable as fuck.

I left my room and closed the door, then I wandered into the kitchen and quickly put some dishes in the dishwasher. I then got rid of the plates, cups, and beer bottles from my living room and dining room and put them in the kitchen. *God, I'm such a slob.*

The doorbell rang just in time. I answered the door to see Talia standing there in a white flowy-looking sundress and those damn cowboy boots that drove me crazy. Her hair was down, the wild curls falling around her face. As usual, she didn't have on much makeup, but her pretty pink lips were all shiny. I felt myself stiffen in my pants.

She walked in and put her arms around me and smiled. "I've missed you."

I chuckled, kissing the top of her head. "You just saw me this morning."

"I know," she laughed. "Are you ready?"

I nodded, patting myself down to make sure I had my keys, phone, and wallet. Check, check, check.

We walked out into the parking area, and when I saw her car parked next to mine, I said, "Your car is locked, right?"

She rolled her eyes and smiled. "Yes, dad."

I grabbed her hand and kissed it. "Don't sass me, or I'll have to spank you."

"Promise?" she asked, a mischievous glint in her pretty eyes.

We walked to the restaurant we'd agreed on earlier. It was only a few blocks from my house, and it was a nice night. She planned on staying over, so her coming to meet me here just made sense.

I held her hand as we walked, the warm night not too hot and not cold, just perfect. She told me some more about her mom and a younger brother who had received a college scholarship and was living somewhere out west to get his degree. I talked to her about my mom and stepdad and told her I wanted her to meet them one day. That made her smile. I finally opened up about my visit with Harper Mathis and the job prospects she'd given me. She looked so happy, I tried to memorize her face.

"Ellis Anderson?"

We turned around slowly when a male voice said my name with an authority I recognized. Two Tampa P.D. officers were standing there, looking stern.

"Yes, sir?"

The larger of the two walked over and pulled out a pair of handcuffs. "Sorry, son, but you're under arrest for assault and battery of Justin Silver."

"Fuck," I muttered. I didn't even need to ask. That pussy bitch Ripper had pressed charges.

"Oh, my God! No, please don't," Talia said, seeming to know why I was being put in cuffs. "That thug attacked us first!"

The shorter of the two officers paused for a

minute, but only said, "Ma'am, please step away, we have to take him in."

Talia was crying now, dammit. The officer took mercy on her and handed her a card. "He's being taken here. He can probably make bail, but call that number and they will let you know."

She took the card but kept looking at me as the cops walked me to their waiting car, putting me into the backseat. I gave no resistance, as I knew they were just doing their job. I could only hope to claim self-defense. There went my chances with the prison job.

Fuck my life...

I turned around to see Talia standing in the street with the glare from the streetlamps illuminating the tears streaming down her cheeks. I swallowed the lump in my throat and shook my head. If that shitbag was out and I'm going to jail, I was gonna find his ass when I make bail and he was gonna face the wrath of LT.

The drive had been short and the booking process very standard. As I lay on a cold, hard bunk in a cell wearing an orange jumpsuit with nothing to entertain me but my thoughts, I wondered if I would ever see Talia again. Assaulted, had a gun pulled on her, now watching me get arrested. Yeah, I was such a catch. At least I'd told her about my past, so I held onto a small glimmer of hope that she would forgive me - again.

God, what a mess I've made. I should have just stayed in the Marines. Why the hell did I get out anyway? Oh yeah, 'cause my body was starting to break down from all the stress and injuries. Plus I was missing home, which obviously made me a pussy. Yep, should have stayed in.

"What the fuck are you doing on that side of the bars, Anderson?"

My head jerked up when I heard his voice. A deep voice I'd know anywhere. A smile I couldn't control spread across my face and I stood, rushing over to the bars. "Duke. What are *you* doing here?"

He pointed to the pretty-boy next to him with the dark hair and a badge attached to his belt. "My brother told me you were here."

"Okay… well are you springing me, Sarge?"

Duke laughed his deep rumbling laugh, one I hadn't heard in years. "Yeah."

I looked a bit confused. I hadn't seen Duke Hawthorne since I'd gotten out a few months ago. I knew he lived here, had gotten himself some badass FBI job years ago, but I had no idea who his brother was. I tilted my head in confusion as I looked at him.

"This is Detective Mason Oliver. He's my brother, like I said. He's with Tampa P.D. He saw you being brought in, but when he learned your name by seeing it on the prisoner list, he recognized it and called me. I told him about how you saved my life in Afghanistan, bro."

"Honored to meet you, Ellis," Mason said, putting his hand through the bars. I put mine out and shook it.

I looked at Duke, then let my chin fall. "I didn't save your life, how many times I gotta tell you that?"

Detective Oliver opened the door with a set of keys attached to his belt and let me out of the cell.

Mason Oliver had kind hazel eyes and a tough exterior, combined with professional pressed clothing that matched his professional attitude. I liked him already. I nodded my appreciation at him for letting me out.

"What time is it?" I asked Duke.

He rubbed a hand over his beard and looked at his fancy watch. "Almost 2 a.m."

Fuck. I'd been sitting in that damn cell for eight hours.

"You posted my bail?" I asked, cringing at the thought of owing anyone anything. I couldn't imagine how much that would cost, and I was obviously still unemployed, living off of my government check for now. I watched as Duke limped slightly and I felt sick that he still had pain from that injury, the one that replayed in my nightmares every night.

"Wish I could be the hero in this story, dude, but I'm not. Your girl is."

I looked at him questioningly. "Talia was here? She posted my bail?"

He shook his head as he pulled out a can of chew and shoved some dip into his bottom lip. "Nah, she just gave her statement to my bro here. She told him how Silver had pulled a gun on you guys in the middle of traffic and that's all we needed to hear."

"His nickname is Ripper, just FYI," I said to Mason.

Mason laughed with his arms still folded across his chest. "Yeah, we know. After he was treated at the hospital, two uniforms brought him in for questioning. We let him go because he left out the part about him pulling a gun on you and Red. After she gave her statement, we checked the traffic cameras, which confirmed her story. We then brought him in on felony gun charges and stripped him before tossing him in a cell. He's got RIPPER tattooed across his entire back. We asked him what it meant, and he told us it's his alias. And he told us fairly easily, I might add." He chuckled.

"Felony gun charges? He didn't actually shoot us..." I trailed off.

"Felon in Possession of a Firearm," Duke said. "He's facing another five years. He can't be in possession of any weapons. Firearms, knives, explosives... all will get him thrown back in prison. Which is where he's headed now... on federal charges this time. There is no parole. He'll do the full five years, plus the three the state let him off. You don't need to worry about that douchebag, Anderson."

To say I was relieved wouldn't be a lie. I wasn't afraid for myself, just my girl. She didn't need to be thrust into this world of mine. Where my past indiscretions were colliding with my present. She didn't deserve that. She deserved to be treated like a queen, and after this horrid experience, I sure as fuck was going to treat her like one.

After out-processing and getting my clothes and personal property back, Mason dropped me off at my house. I had debated having him drop me at Talia's, but it was 4 a.m., and wasn't sure that was a good idea. Exhaustion overtook me and I thought maybe a few hours of sleep would do me good, so I gave him my address instead. I barely made it to my room once inside, and the minute my head hit the pillow, I was out like a light, my final thoughts on how I was going to go see my girl tomorrow and make everything okay again.

If that was even possible.

Chapter 14

Talia

School passed quickly the next day, and I aced my first geometry exam of the new semester. I was very proud of myself for doing it, even if I had nobody to share my elation with. Thoughts of Ellis invaded my brain at least once an hour, but I was glad I'd not let the thoughts of last night consume me to the point of failing my exam. Even more than that, thoughts of the other big news I'd received yesterday.

Yes, I'd gone down to the precinct to give my statement. I was beyond pissed off that they'd arrested him for assault when that disgusting Ripper guy had pulled out a gun in the middle of broad daylight - and had threatened me with it. I just had to do something. So I did. I'd gone back to his house and got in my car. I then marched my ass into that police station and demanded to talk to someone.

They'd kept me waiting in that uncomfortable waiting area for over an hour, but eventually, an extremely hot cop named Detective Oliver in a pressed blue shirt and slacks with black hair and the coolest hazel eyes I had ever seen came in and took my statement. He was so hot, it was kinda distracting, I'm not gonna lie. But he was no Ellis. This guy was a bit pretty, unlike my rugged man. I told Detective Oliver about how that disgusting piece of shit had pulled a gun from the back of his baggy pants and had pointed it at me and forced me out of the car.

He had asked if I wanted to press charges for assault and hostage-taking. I'd said yes. So yay me, now I get to go to court and testify against that douche-canoe. The detective then punched some keys on his computer and pulled up a grainy traffic camera. I watched in awe as the scene that wouldn't stop replaying in my brain replayed on his computer screen. Just how I'd remembered it. He'd thanked me for my time and then told me I could go.

But what bothered me the most was how they wouldn't let me see Ellis while I was there. They said a judge had to decide on bail and that visiting hours were at noon the next day. Discouraged, I'd left the police station to try to get some rest, knowing I had tests today. And I was glad I'd had. There was nothing more I could do. Plus, I was exhausted beyond belief. I just worried about Ellis being in jail and hoped he was safe.

I shoved the key into the lock to my apartment and flung open the door. Throwing my purse and keys onto the dining room table, I picked up Misty and kissed the top of her furry head. She meowed loudly when she had had enough cuddles and I put her down on the floor and went into the bathroom. I avoided eye contact with the little white stick that showed two pink lines still sitting on the back of the toilet. If I didn't acknowledge that it wasn't real, it wouldn't be, right? The problem would just go away and I could get on with my life. So that's what I did. Those drug-store tests were wrong all the time anyway.

Sighing in denial, I went into the living room and plopped down on the sofa, wondering when I would be able to see Ellis again. How long was he going to spend in jail? My stomach turned over and I gagged and almost threw up thinking about him sitting in a cold cell.

Or perhaps there was another reason for the nausea…

I shifted my thoughts.

It was almost 2 in the afternoon and I had the evening off from the coffee shop. My classes were done for the week and I wondered what I should do to keep my mind off of all this shit. I smiled again when I thought of the test I'd aced – not the one in the bathroom but the one in the college classroom – and my immediate response was to call my mom to tell her. But my mom wasn't around for me to call. She'd died along with my heart when she'd overdosed on a cocaine-tequila cocktail on my 21st birthday.

I shook my head, trying not to remember her

open, milky eyes and the white foam bubbling from the side of her mouth. I'd come home from school that day in a great mood, hoping for a birthday present. Instead I'd received a reoccurring nightmare that would probably plague me for the rest of my eternal freaking days.

I used the remote to pop the TV on and stared without seeing at the late afternoon talk show. Another TV psych trying to help a young girl from going down the wrong path. With my arms folded over my chest, I just shook my head at this guy, thinking he could fix this young girl. Little did he know – he couldn't. She would be fucked up for life unless she made her own conscious decision to turn in a different direction and make things better for herself. I turned the TV off and decided to visit Mom.

I parked in the lot that could use some new asphalt and got out of my small car. In my left hand, I clutched the small bouquet of multi-colored flowers I'd picked up at the grocery store. In my right hand, my car keys were gripped tightly. I took a deep breath and headed toward the headstone that was so familiar it shouldn't cause me pain anymore.

But it always did.

I slogged over felled leaves and wet earth until I reached it. I placed the flowers at the foot of the headstone and sat cross-legged in front of it.

SHARON MARIE SMITH-LOGAN

1969 - 2014

Mother, wife, friend, angel

With a deep sigh, I said, "Hi, mom."

The cold, gray stone said nothing in return.

"I wish you were here. I need some advice on a boy."

Inhaling a deep breath, I continued. "Mom, he's so beautiful, he takes my breath away. His eyes are the color of the sky on a perfectly clear day, and they stare at me - they stare *through* me. I can get lost in them for days." I laughed lightly without humor, plucking a few blades of grass from beside me. "I suppose I sound like a total sap." With another deep sigh, I kept talking to no one, the confessions somehow feeling like a deep cleansing of my soul. "I'm pretty sure I love him. But how can I love someone who's bad for me? He's bad, Mama. He's so very bad. He's got a bad past, and he's done some awful things. He can't be good for me, right?"

A horn honking knocked me out of my whispered confessions to my long-dead mother. I looked up to see nothing in the parking lot.

Shaking my head at my foolishness, I kept rambling. "He's so beautiful, Mom. His voice is deep and his mouth is perfect. When I kiss him, I get lost in his, his… well, his everything. I try to keep my eyes open to capture the breathtaking blue of his eyes but they end up drifting closed so I can get lost in him. And when his rough hands turn soft and explore my every inch, I am completely useless. I turn to putty in his hands."

A slight warm breeze blew. I closed my eyes, pretending it was my mother, coming to offer me a sliver of comfort or advice as to what I should do about Ellis. My mind wanted to hate him - to tell him to get out of my life. It would be so much simpler if I didn't have all this drama. But my heart… it tightened painfully in my chest and begged me to go to him. Like a magnet. He was the negative charge and I was the positive, drawn together inexplicably and it was infuriatingly unexplainable.

I shook my head. "What does all this mean, Mama? Should I just fall into him, let him have me - let me have him, any way I can get him? Or should I tell him to move on without me? Aside from being beautiful, he's also got something deep inside of him that seems like it needs to be let out. I want to help him exorcise his demons. I want him to open up more to me. And he has, to an extent. I want to be and have been sympathetic to his troubles while trying to let him know I need him to help me through my trials, too. What do I do? Why aren't you here to help me with this? Why did you have to leave?" I choked on a strangled sob and wiped tears from my cheeks, trying to breathe through the pain in my throat and chest at her loss. I sniffled like a child and took a deep breath. "You were so selfish, you know. You should have thought about me and Calvin before you left us. Even though we're adults, we still need you. Why couldn't you see that? Understand that?"

I plucked some more grass and threw it angrily onto the ground. Then I looked back at the cold, gray engraved stone. "What do I do? Please, just tell me." I sobbed into my hands, feeling lost, and almost crazy.

"You choose love," a voice said from behind me.

I turned around to see Ellis standing there, all smugness and cockiness gone from his face. His hands were in the pockets of his jeans and the black *Wounded Warrior Foundation* T-shirt fit snugly over his chest. His face was a mixture of curiosity and warmth, and my knees went weak.

"How..." I asked, the words trapped in my throat as I stared at his beautiful figure. He was a vision, gorgeous and breathtaking, and I was powerless to resist him.

But then I thought - why and how had he

thought to look here of all places? I couldn't ever recall telling him where my mom had been laid to rest but maybe one time I'd had? There had been a few nights where the wine had been flowing and perhaps my loose lips had gotten the better of me. Regardless – he was here now, so what was I going to say to him?

So I swiped at another tear but stayed seated. "How long have you been standing there?"

A serious countenance darkened his face, and his jaw ticked. "Long enough."

I sucked in a breath and let it out. "That's not an answer."

"I don't give two fucks, sweetheart," he whispered, gliding over to me and offering a hand. "Let's get out of here."

I didn't move, but stared up at him incredulously. "Just like that? You just want me to leave with you after hearing all that?"

He smiled a little. "Yes, leave with me. Be with me. Stay with me. Live with me. Marry me. I'll take care of you. I can be everything you were confessing to your mom and more. I've made peace with my past and I think you should, too." He nodded to the tombstone and looked back to me. "Talia, I'm going to be the man you need. To be the man I want to be. The man who's going to be a daddy to our baby."

He stared down at me, his hand still outstretched. I forgot to breathe as I looked up at him. "How... how did you know?"

Without breaking eye contact, he pulled out my pregnancy test stick from his pants pocket and held it up, smiling. "I went looking for you. You didn't lock your apartment door, T. You should be more careful. This caught my eye in the bathroom."

A single tear dripped down my face and I looked up at him. "Do you mean all that stuff you just said?"

Nodding, he smiled a little, pulling me to stand. He reached his hand up to my face, his thumb swiping away my sadness. "Of course. I love you, Talia. I always have. You just couldn't see it because I was too selfish and stupid to tell you, to show you. And for that I'm sorry."

His fingers brushed slightly over my belly and his eyes shifted down to it. "I love you. I'm gonna marry you, and we're gonna give that kid a great life, better than the one we had. You in, sweetheart?"

I smiled through my tears. "Yeah, baby. I'm in. For life."

The End

Partial proceeds of this books in this series will go to *Honor the Sacrifice*. You can donate, too! God bless the troops! www.honor-the-sacrifice.org

Above Protection

(Imperfect Heroes Series) is Book 2

Meet Special Agent Duke Hawthorne

Song List:

Zero - Chris Brown
Rage - Hyper Crush
The Man I Want To Be - Chris Young
Big Girls Cry - Sia
Love In The Dark - Adele
Not About Angels - Birdy
Sugar - Robin Schultz
Faction 02 - Celldweller
Monster - Skillet
Shameless - Garth Brooks
I Don't Dance - Lee Brice
Call Your Name - Daughtry
She Rides Away - David Nail
I'm Coming Over -Chris Young
Heart Of Stone - Iko
Hell On An Angel - Brantley Gilbert
Cold - Aqualung & Lucy Schwartz
Heartbeat - Carrie Underwood
Live Until I Die - Clay Walker
Tryin' To Love Me - Jason Aldean
If It Don't Take Two - Shania Twain
Just A Game - Birdy
Beautiful Drug - Zac Brown Band
Turning Page - Sleeping At Last
You Should Be Here - Cole Swindell
Like A Cowboy - Randy Houser

About the Author

C.J. is a USA Today Bestselling author living in Colorado. Lover of red wine, wearer of fabulous shoes, and a die-hard Niner fan, she's also an editor at heart. She's written over a dozen books and short stories that contain both contemporary/new adult and paranormal romance that are a little bit badass, a little heart-wrenching, and sorta funny (to her, anyway). Almost all of her books usually contain law enforcement or military undertones, since strong, brave, alpha men and women are her weaknesses. When she's not writing, she can be found working at a very strange day job, which may or may not have some mild influences on her gripping stories – so strange, in fact, she may just write a book about it one day.

She's also a proud member of the Romance Writers of America (RWA).

Find her on Facebook, Twitter, Goodreads, and on her website, www.cjpinard.com

C.J. pinard

USA Today Bestselling Author

mystery ♥ magic ♥ magnetism

CPSIA information can be obtained
at www.ICGtesting.com
Printed in the USA
BVOW06s0153150317
478558BV00009B/104/P

9 781523 651566